Craving Dr. Silver Fox

An Age-Gap, Grumpy Sunshine, Off-limits Romance

Judy Hale

Copyright © 2024 by Judy Hale

All rights reserved.

No portion of this book may be reproduced, distributed, or transmitted in any form or by any means including photocopying, recording, copy-pasting, screenshots, or other electronic or mechanical methods without prior written permission of the copyright owner listed above, except in brief quotations embodied in critical reviews and certain other non-commercial uses as permitted by copyright law.

This is a work of fiction. Any resemblance to persons, names, characters, organizations, brands, and actual events is either purely coincidental or a product of the author's vivid imagination.

Contents

	Playlist	V
		VII
1.	Prologue	1
2.	Chapter One	14
3.	Chapter Two	21
4.	Chapter Three	30
5.	Chapter Four	37
6.	Chapter Five	51
7.	Chapter Six	58
8.	Chapter Seven	66
9.	Chapter Eight	80
10.	Chapter Nine	93

11.	Chapter Ten	110
12.	Chapter Eleven	120
13.	Chapter Twelve	122
14.	Chapter Thirteen	131
15.	Chapter Fourteen	143
16.	Chapter Fifteen	151
17.	Chapter Sixteen	155
18.	Chapter Seventeen	168
19.	Chapter Eighteen	173
20.	Chapter Nineteen	177
21.	Chapter Twenty	187
22.	Chapter Twenty-One	190
23.	Chapter Twenty-Two	199
24.	Chapter Twenty-Three	206
25.	Chapter Twenty-Four	213
26.	Chapter Twenty-Five	215
27.	Chapter Twenty-Six	222
28.	Epilogue	231
	Acknowledgements	240
	About the Author	241
	Also By Judy Hale	242

Playlist

LISTEN ON SPOTIFY

You Say — Lauren Daigle
Fire on Fire — Sam Smith
Older — Isabel LaRosa
Fool For You — ZAYN
Call Out My Name — The Weeknd
Under The Influence — Chris Brown

You saved me, even when I didn't know it...

Prologue

TESSA

FIVE YEARS AGO

"Can I sit here?" I point at the mouth-watering pair of thighs encased in black cotton, with muscles bulging in all the right places.

I never imagined I'd be saying those words. Especially not here in the small town of Valencia, at the Annual Citrus Fest, with hundreds of people close by.

Certainly not to the impossibly gorgeous man sprawled on a sturdy lawn chair that seems way too small for his bulky frame. He sips on some citrus concoction and stares pensively off into the tranquil lake.

Nathan King.

He's the reason I came back despite promising myself I never would when I walked out on my dad last year.

I look down at him again and my heart skips a beat. The top few buttons of his black shirt are undone, drawing my eyes to the tanned skin peeking through the opening.

It's dark out here and his face is partly covered in my shadow, but I don't need to see it. I already know what he looks like with his piercing blue eyes and a strong stubbled jaw that I'd do anything to feel against my cheek.

He's a doctor, and one of the most famous oncologists in the States, but he could also make a killing as a movie star.

I realized during my pre-med year that having a crush on a famous doctor, however renowned, was a stupid reason to study medicine. So, I quickly changed my major to something I'm truly passionate about: non-profit work.

That didn't douse my ardor, though. He's still the sexiest man I've ever seen.

Unfortunately, he's also one I shouldn't be crushing on. Because he's twenty years my senior, my self-appointed mentor, and most importantly, my dad hates his guts.

I wonder if Nathan knows about that last part.

I step to the side so that lights from the booths in the distance can illuminate his face, which I note is devoid of expression.

Only the pause of the bottle on the way to his mouth gives away his surprise at my request.

Well, at least I managed to surprise the unflappable Dr. King.

"You want to sit where?" His deep voice rumbles incredulously.

My cheeks flame hotter. "Um, on your lap?" I squeak.

I swear it sounded a lot less insane in my head two minutes ago. And three weeks ago, I agreed with Isa, my best friend, that it was brilliant idea when she suggested I make a move on Nathan.

Although whatever happened to good old 'hello' or even 'can I buy you another cocktail?'

Must be the darkness and perhaps the zesty citrus cocktail in my hand that's making me this bold. *Or this stupid.*

He gestures to the empty chair beside him. "There happens to be a perfectly good seat right here. Why would you want to sit on me, Tess?"

His eyes tell me that he already knows the answer, he just wants me to spell it out.

The look he gives me sends a jolt through me, ending in an inexplicable urge to run, but I stay put as he cocks his head to one side to study me.

For the first time in the five years I've known him, I see his gaze shift from amiable and professional respect to something else entirely. It's intense, an unmistakable spark of heat as it sweeps over me. Attraction?

Wishful thinking?

In any case, it's too late to back out now. I've come on to him. I have to stick it out.

Isa's words echo in my mind.

You're a grown woman, and a gorgeous one at that. And he's a single, red-blooded, straight man with eyes in his head.

She's right. I can do this.

I'm no longer that geeky teen his hospital gifted with a fancy stethoscope for helping kids with cancer.

I'm an adult, I'm bold and I've got a plan.

I make myself hold his gaze, then run my fingers through my curly blonde hair – a move that usually makes guys at college do a double-take. In try for a sultry voice, but with my nerves I'm pretty sure I sound more like a strangled cat.

"Because I want to, Dr. King."

Cringe. Oh my God, kill me now.

I hazard a look down at Nathan again and catch something flash in his eyes. He says nothing for the longest time, merely watches me with interest. And just when I think he's about to send me away like a naughty child, he finally huffs out an amused breath, then leans back and slowly spreads his legs wide.

"Have at it, Tess."

Heat engulfs my face as my mouth goes dry. Suddenly, those four words are the most provocative ones I've ever heard. *Ever*.

What have I done?

I'm not sure what I expected when I came on to him. But it was not him reclining his big body and inviting me to sample his six plus feet of muscle heaven.

I pause, looking back at the rest of the town milling about a hundred yards away. Granted, this area is a secluded spot. Heavy foliage from the trees lining the grassy bank of the lake obscures us from casual viewing. Still, someone could see.

And they'll undoubtedly talk.

He cocks a thick eyebrow in challenge when he sees my hesitation. "What's the matter, Tess?"

Exactly, what's the matter, Theresa? Isn't this why you came all the way from Boston?

My inner voice of insanity makes a valid point. But fantasizing and actually experiencing the fantasy up close are two different things.

It's been a year since I last saw him. It should have been plenty of time to forget my stupid crush. Only, it wasn't.

Which was why I thought I'd take Isa's advice and infuse a dash of reality in hopes of drowning my crush. After all, things– and people– hardly live up to the mind's flowery expectations.

So, with that in mind, I made plans to attend the Annual Citrus Fest because I knew he'd be here. This is one event he never misses.

Our town was named after the Valencia orange, a nod to its history with the fruit and its abundance of orange orchards. That's why the Annual Citrus Fest means a lot to someone like Nathan, who was born and raised here.

Every year, he gives a speech at the fest. After that, he wanders alone over to this pier. He sits for a while before returning to LA.

I suspect this lakefront holds some sentimental value to him, although I'm not quite sure why.

Nathan's eyes rake over me again. There's no doubt: his stare is carnal. It makes me bold enough to take up his invitation.

Besides, he can't possibly feel as good as he looks, can he?

So, with my heart pounding, I put my drink on the ground next to his chair. Then, I lower myself into the space between his thighs.

The first thing that hits me is his warmth, followed by the smell of his skin.

Earth and man.

I close my eyes against the unexpected shock of pleasure that leaves me wanting more. I can't resist reclining back against his broad chest.

Which now leaves my hands. Where do I put them?

Should I tuck them against my body? Lift my arms over my head and link my fingers together at his nape?

Finally, I decide to place them over his thighs. The moment they touch him, my fingers involuntarily flex against hard muscle.

Holy shit, does the man live in the gym or something?

Nathan lets out a small sound. It could be surprise or disgruntlement, but I'm too busy soaking in his nearness to care.

Then he bends to whisper right in my ear, even though it's just the two of us out here. "So, tell me, Tess, what are you playing at?"

The masculine energy brimming from him makes my head feel wooly. Without thinking, I inch my butt against his crotch so I'm rubbing up against him. Another shock of pleasure runs through me as I feel him through his pants.

I'm actually doing this!

He feels large, but he's not exactly hard.

I'm the slightest bit disappointed that he's *that* unbothered while I'm about to combust. I'm also intrigued by his lack of a physical reaction.

Since getting to college and discovering how, with a few practiced poses, I could easily have guys panting with desire, I can't remember having had to work this hard to get a guy all over me.

I'm sure if I tried what I'm doing to his crotch right now on one of those poor college boys, they'd have come in their pants by now.

Must be because Nathan is older, a fact which excites me to no end.

When I continue to brush against him like a cat, he snaps, "Tess!" His voice cracks like a whip, making me pause.

"What?" I purr back, my voice a blend of sultry and mock innocence. "I just want to talk."

"We talked earlier." He reminds me.

He's right. He gave a speech during the fest and I caught him right after for a mentor-mentee chat.

"Yes, and we kept getting interrupted every five seconds," I protest "I just want to continue our deep, intellectual conversation."

"Then, sit still and use your mouth," he commands, his voice firm, sending an unexpected thrill through me.

"Sure," I reply, attempting to sound obedient. But the moment I try to settle, my body has other ideas, betraying me with its restless rhythm.

This time, his hands capture my arms to keep me still. Then comes his chuckle, a sound so warm it sends shivers down my spine, even though I can tell his laughter isn't entirely from amusement.

"Do you have something in your pants, Tess?"

I lean back, loving the heat of his breath on my ear. "Maybe I do, or maybe I'm just allergic to sitting still. It's one of those rare conditions, I'm sure you know about it."

Instead of the flirty retort I expect, his voice suddenly goes gruff as he whispers, "But why, Tess?"

My brows lift in question although he can't see my face. "Why what?"

His voice goes even softer, to the point where it's almost inaudible. "Why are you doing this, little girl?"

I blink, momentarily distracted from seeking my pleasure. I've done this countless times over the past year, since Mom's death, and I've never had to answer that question before.

Also, having him label me as a "little girl" rankles.

Like he still sees me as that awkward teenager who hung on to his every word.

I'm almost twenty-one.

And he's forty.

So? I want to kick that snarky voice in the mouth.

To Nathan I say, "Don't call me little girl."

He must hear the irritation lacing my tone because his body softens against mine, and his grip on my arms loosens.

He chuckles, "You're right, Tess. You're not a little girl anymore. That much is crystal clear." Then his voice drops an octave lower and he murmurs, "So baby girl, why do you want me?"

Baby girl. Holy fuck yes.

Wetness pools at my core as my nails reflexively score his thighs. I wanted to seduce Nathan, but it looks like my plan just backfired.

"Nathan," I murmur silkily, not exactly sure what I'm about to ask him for this time.

However, he goes rigid the moment I say his name. His heart starts to pound against my back, and his breathing changes.

I wonder if it's my sultry tone or the sound of his name that's putting him in this state. I suspect it's the latter since I've been speaking this way all night, but I've never called him by his first name before.

So I decide to try it again.

Throwing my head back on his shoulder, I whisper his name against his jaw. And sure enough, the tempo of his heart rate picks up.

He likes it! It's like he can't even help his reaction.

And I grow even slicker between my legs with the knowledge that I can have such an effect on a man like him.

Nathan takes what feels like a few calming breaths, then growls, "You're playing a dangerous game, Tess, you know that?"

He pulls me flush against his crotch, and I gasp.

He's hard as steel. And huge. Suddenly, my skin feels too tight, and my core throbs. I clench my thighs and bite my bottom lip to suppress the moan threatening to escape.

Right now, I'm so turned on that I can hardly see straight. I don't think there's anything I wouldn't be prepared to do to get him to fuck me tonight.

As though reading my mind, he growls into my ear, "You're delectable, Tess. But I'm not going to fuck you just because you're too scared to deal with your own emotions."

"What?" My fog of arousal lifts, getting replaced by a knot of dread for what he'll say next.

"You want to wash away the painful memories right? So that when you think of Valencia, all you'll remember is the thrill of the taboo fuck you had with an older man. Instead of how your mother died and how your father couldn't care less."

His words rain over me like freezing water, drowning every ounce of desire I felt seconds ago.

Of course he's heard about my mom. Rumors were rife about the pathetic rich man's wife who was so deranged that she ended up taking her own life.

The one whose husband couldn't wait to move on with his next squeeze.

Pain lances at me again for what Mom suffered as my dad's wife.

What *I* suffered trying to pour myself into the John Blackwell mold.

Everything the Blackwells did was news that got spread around Valencia, including adopting me at the age of eleven.

Just when I was beginning to settle down into my new, if somewhat strange, family, Mom's curious death and my dad's indiscretions became gossip fodder for everyone else. Cruel whispers and speculations surged.

But not one single person had brought her up to me with this level of insensitivity.

And to think it would come from the one person who always had nothing but encouragement and unwavering faith in me and my abilities is soul-crushing.

I yank myself off him, standing stiffly with my back turned, my arms going around myself as if to protect me from his words.

"I'm not scared of *anything*," I snap, staring unseeingly into the glassy water.

He stands up, too, then comes around to face me.

"Aren't you? Because I've watched you grow up, Tess. I see how brilliant you are out in the world, yet you struggle to find a place at home."

I instantly regret telling him about my family.

On one of those days in my junior year of high school, my charity team had a fundraising meeting with Nathan, whom we'd appointed as a patron.

He'd seen me fighting to hold back tears throughout the meeting, and then he got me alone demanding to know what the problem was.

I'd been so overwhelmed that I'd needed no hard prompting before I told him everything, sobbing all the way through my explanation.

Nathan held my hand and promised me that I was going to be okay in spite of my family.

His gruff voice dissipates those memories now. "Did you think coming back here and doing something shocking will be enough to erase what this place reminds you of?"

He bends closer to me when I don't respond. "Newsflash, Tess: nothing erases the pain, not unless you grow a pair and face it head-on like an adult."

Tears spring to my eyes and my fingers start to tremble as I fold them into fists. I want to rage at him. To tell him to go to hell.

But I can't.

Because he's right.

He's right about most things, except why I came back.

Sure, I was tired of crushing on him from afar, but more than that, I just needed to see him.

Because ever since the day he made me that promise and shared his tough times growing up working in orchards, Nathan's been like a grounding force for me.

This past year, I've made some big changes. I stopped talking to my dad because I realized he had no use for me after Mom died. Also, I switched from UCLA pre-med to a non-profit management program in Boston, all on my own.

Isa and her brother Chris, were there for me, but I needed someone like Nathan.

Someone who's been through rough patches and could tell me that it was going to be okay.

After his speech today, I intended to ask him out for drinks, but he seemed distracted, like he couldn't even remember me.

He continues standing beside me, his big body radiating warmth against my suddenly chilly skin. His nearness is like a bed of roses—enticing in its beauty, yet laced with vicious thorns.

I take a deep breath, square my shoulders, and face him, my eyes bright with defiance as I mentally steel myself to hear more.

He can't be half as horrible as my dad, who is an expert in verbally reducing people to ashes.

I find Nathan watching me intently as the tiniest bit of emotion seeps into his eyes.

"You want my advice?" he asks.

Not really, no.

I can't bring myself to answer.

"Go *away*. Your mother is gone. There's nothing holding you back anymore. You're brilliant, Tess. Why not invest your energy into your career and into people who actually give a shit about you?"

He leans over to brush a kiss across my forehead, and I cringe, unable to take his tenderness after his words have ripped me to shreds. He holds his body away from mine, then has an unreadable expression in his eyes.

"Night, Tess. I wish you the best."

With those parting words, he walks away.

I stand rooted on the spot, not even turning to watch him leave.

Tears fill my eyes and spill down my cheeks. I let them fall, and soon enough, a sob wrenches itself out of my throat. I double over from the pain, giving myself over to it.

I've spent the last year running from the truth that I'm utterly alone in the world. I tried everything to escape the pain; I had gotten into drinking, smoking, and hooking up with random guys, but nothing seemed to work long-term.

Maybe like Nathan said, facing that truth will make life easier to bear.

Like an adult.

He treated me like a snotty child. I feel the sharp talons of mortification reaching for me and savagely yanking out the pathetic crush I've been nursing for Nathan King. One I've been unable to get rid of.

That crush made me travel six hours, digging into my meager savings so I could see his face and talk to him again.

Invest your energy into people who actually give a shit about you.

Apparently, he doesn't.

But in some twisted way, that's exactly what I needed to hear to let go of the one final tie I thought, I had to this place.

The past decade has shown me that the one thing I've always wanted, belonging to a family, just isn't all that it's cracked up to be.

So, I'm going to throw myself out into the world and make it remember my name.

As an added bonus, I would never need to see Nathan King again.

Chapter One

TESSA

PRESENT DAY

"Thank you for coming on such short notice." Detective Warner's voice is pitchy, and his fingers tremble as he fumbles around with the case files on his desk.

I mask my irritation, wondering if he's ill-prepared for this meeting or just plain ill, judging from the shakiness. Not exactly the kind of person I want handling my mom's case.

But then, beggars can't be choosers. That the major crimes unit of the Valencia police department decided to reopen Mom's case at all is something.

Maybe I can finally get the closure that has eluded me for six years.

find myself back in Valencia, a town I vowed never to return to.

"It's not a problem," I tell the detective, even though it is.

It's a huge problem. It looks like I'll be stuck here, just in time for my dad's wedding.

He's been through a string of girlfriends since Mom passed six years ago, but now getting married to Joyce Wilcox, a woman in her fifties who's been on TV.

She's striking for her age, but not his usual type. He tends to prefer shy, young, docile heiresses. Joyce is none of those things except for the heiress part.

Mom, on the other hand, was all of those things except that her family was dirt poor.

Whether Dad's taste has changed or it's Joyce's wealth motivating him, I can't tell.

In any case word will get out about me being back, and skipping my father's wedding would stir up more gossip. Not that I care what folks think, but Dad does.

John Blackwell is all about keeping up appearances.

I tell myself I don't give a shit what he thinks anymore since I haven't seen or spoken to him in five years.

Yet, deep down, a part of me that I still haven't managed to bury would hate to embarrass him.

"None of us expected this, you know." Detective Warner flashes me a tight smile as he finally finds the case file he's been looking for, and settles down in his seat. "I mean, it's been six years since she died..."

I flinch as goosebumps rise on my skin. I don't know if I'll *ever* be able to hear about my mom's death without a chill running through my body.

"I'm sorry," Warner says, no doubt seeing my reaction to his statement. "I know it's a touchy subject."

"It's not." My voice conveys a firmness I don't feel.

It *shouldn't* be touchy. I've come a long way from drowning my grief in alcohol and meaningless sex and have done very well for myself.

The co-op program was my ticket to Northeastern University without relying on my dad's money, but it extended my college years.

Now, in the last stretch of my work experience, Guardian Angels Network, the NGO I work with, have already offered me a senior role for after graduation.

So, I've done even better than I thought I would when I cried my eyes out five years ago on that wooden pier after Nathan King told me to leave.

Nathan.

My heart thuds painfully. Although I'd long stopped crushing on the man, his words had hung over me through the years, pushing me to work harder to prove myself.

They caused me to question my motives every time I flirted or hooked up with a random guy until I couldn't bear to do it anymore.

Perhaps that was also why I'd found the strength to return when the police called.

I'm ready to confront my past, even if it means staying in this detested town.

Warner looks like he doesn't believe my claim that I don't find the subject touchy, but he doesn't argue.

"I'll cut right to the chase." He says. "A few months after your dad sold the house, the new owner found some journals in the basement that he thought might interest us."

Warner pulls open a case file and fingers a paper that looks like a copy of a lined journal. "I think you should read this."

Instantly recognizing the handwriting as my mom's, I reach for the paper with trembling fingers, then stare down at the words for a little longer, before I start to register what they say.

October 2nd

Every day, I think back on everything. None of this should have happened. It's all my fault. I was too weak.

Now, the curtain is drawing to a close. Dee keeps telling me that he is waiting for me, and I'm starting to believe him. It's not true, but I can't help believing.

He says that Black will sit on the balcony to watch me. Most nights, it's hard to sleep. Because once I close my eyes, I'll dream of him talking. And talking.

I have a feeling that I'll be gone soon.

It's probably for the best. But if I go and Tessa asks questions, he'll play those deadly games again.

I let the paper flutter to the desk.

"What?" I croak. "What does this mean?"

Warner's expression is grave. "That note was dated two months before she died. There are dozens of entries like that. We haven't quite gotten through all of it yet, but we'll release them into your possession once we're done."

Warner thumbs through a few of the journals as if to emphasize his next words. "Her words are full of metaphors, especially towards the end of her life, and it's very difficult for someone who doesn't know her to figure out what she meant. Or her writings could be the result of being disturbed. Either way, the bottom line is that we are concerned."

He taps the case file. "They suggest that her death may not have been an accident as the inquest ruled."

Or a suicide as the whispers suggested.

My heart misses a beat. "No."

No way.

Six years ago, Mom fell from the balcony of her room and tumbled onto the asphalt below. She wasn't found until morning when my dad returned from one of his long nights out.

He had a rock-solid, if very controversial, alibi: He'd been with another woman the time it happened.

The balcony floor was wooden and it'd been raining at the time, so it was assumed that she'd slipped while tending to her plants. She had possibly been leaning over to reach the overgrown vines, because next to her body was her watering can.

The only snag was that forensics put the time of her fall at about two in the morning. A very unusual time to be tending to plants. But then again, she was an unusual woman.

And now, these journals suggest that there could be more to her death and that she'd been afraid for me.

What did she mean by me asking questions?
What questions would I ask?
Who was going to play what games?

My brain whizzes with possible scenarios. Is it possible Mom was pushed off that balcony by an intruder?

"We need to ask you some questions," Warner says now. "We know your father was out of the house for most of the day and the night of her death and that you were at college."

Out of the house. That's a nice way of putting it, I suppose.

He continues, "So, we thought that between the two of you, we could get enough information to assist with the case and–"

Assist. My mind paints a disturbing picture of my dad and me, sifting through Mom's private journals with me reliving mom's pain while enduring my dad's scorn and impatience.

My dad used to be my favorite person in the world, but all that changed over time, and my passion for charity work annoyed the hell out of him.

He didn't like the idea of me studying medicine, but he really flew off the handle when I informed him that I was leaving UCLA for Boston *and* changing my major to non-profit management.

Since then, things have gotten considerably cooler between us.

We don't speak now, even though he keeps sending invitations for me to come to Thanksgiving, which I think is weird, but knowing my dad, he's probably just doing it to keep up appearances.

Could my dad have gotten someone to do it?

He had no reason to kill Mom. She never questioned his affairs. And she had no money he would inherit. No family or pedigree.

She was already a sad, tortured woman. Why would anyone want to kill her? A shard of white hot pain hits me and I take a deep breath, releasing it slowly.

I thought I was strong enough to face this. I was wrong. Because this is so much worse.

I jerk to my feet. "I can't do this."

Warner looks up at me with furrowed brows. "Ms. Blackwell, I understand that this is very upsetting, but we need you to go through some of these papers. We've made copies for both yourself and Mr. Blackwell to review."

He hands me a blue, plastic ring-bound folder, and although I feel a modicum of relief that my dad and I wouldn't be doing it together, I rear back as though Warner's offering me poison.

Warner urges, "Ms. Blackwell, this has a chance of becoming a real case, and we need as much information as we can get about–"

My phone starts to ring, interrupting him. I yank it from my pocket, relief flooding through me.

I'll take any other conversation over one more second of reliving my mother's death.

I glance at my phone screen, barely registering the name of the caller, then say to the detective, "I'm sorry, but I have to take this, it's work."

Warner opens his mouth to protest, but I dash out of his office and into the small, carpeted hallway that leads outside the police precinct before he can say anything more.

As if the phone call can save me from what I need to do.

Chapter Two

TESSA

I PUSH OPEN THE heavy front door of the Valencia police station and step into the balmy fall breeze. I pick up the still ringing phone and press it next to my ear.

"Hi, Zara."

"Tessa!" Zara, my work colleague from Guardian Angels Network, sounds as cheery as usual. Her bubbly mood usually lifts mine, but today, I feel tears spring to my eyes as I hear her voice.

What I wouldn't give to be back in my little cubicle at the office, exchanging small talk and listening as Zara prattles on about the latest office gossip.

"Hi," I say again, this time in the most chirpy tone I can manage. "How's it going?"

"You know," she begins, "I went for a meeting with Opal Superstores this morning. Turns out, they can't pay for what they ordered. I'm having to reassess what we can offer within the budget they're proposing, the negotiations for which should have ended with my coffee in their branch manager's sexy as hell face given the price he's offering."

A wan smile tugs at my lips. "It's going great, then. So, did the sexy as hell manager throw in a sweetener?" I keep walking until I reach the side of the building, away from prying eyes.

Taking another gulp of fresh air, I then lean on the cool, gray stone wall of the Valencia PD building, happy to let Zara suck me into the mundane workings of Guardian Angels Network, if only to delay the inevitable waiting for me inside the station.

"You know it." Zara's cheery tone warms me. "He's buying me a proper coffee later today. Not that it'll do much for him, but I'll take whatever he's offering."

I laugh. Zara is as stubborn as a mule.

"How's it going over there, anyway?" Zara asks. "Is your small town exactly the way you left it?"

She was raised in Boston, so she finds the idea of a small town fascinating.

I shrug, more to give myself something to do than anything else. "More or less."

Actually, no, so many things have changed. Even Lake Orange is now sporting a spectacular restaurant built right on the pier.

The same pier that Nathan likes to sit on once a year.

No one in Boston knows much about my life here. I only told work folks that I needed to visit my dad.

"So, how long are you planning to stay out there for?" Zara asks. "I know townies always go on about how they *hate* being back in their hometowns. But when you go back, nothing seems to be able to pull you out."

I look back at the looming building behind me. For a fraction of a second, I'm terrified that Zara's prediction may come to pass.

That I'll never be able to leave here.

The sooner I can find the strength to carry the weight of that binder, the sooner I'm out of here.

Something tells me it's not until I return to Boston, safely cocooned in my apartment and away from the vicious tongues of Valencia, would I have the courage to get into the contents of those journals.

"Not this townie, dear. I'll be back in a few days." Enough time for the detectives to know which direction the case is heading.

"Are you really sure about that, girl?"

"Why, what do you mean?"

"Well," she begins, and I can picture her taking a sip of her usual caramel latte while she prepares to give me the latest. "We heard something off the radar, babe."

By "off the radar," she means Betty, the Guardian Angels Network director's elderly secretary.

Betty is phenomenal, if a little hard of hearing. She more than makes up for that with how much she talks, which is a nice balance to our director, who seems to delight in hoarding information until the very last minute.

"Tell me." I know this gossip is going to be good based on how mischevious Zara's tone has become.

"It sounds like your pet project is taking off sooner than we thought."

"My pet project? Zara, my proposal has already been adopted by the community center," I remind her, not quite getting her meaning.

When I started with Guardian Angels three months ago, I'd submitted two proposals to Walter Heche, the NGO's director, in hopes that one of them might be selected as a viable project.

One of my proposals was adopted within the first month and, surprisingly, already gaining traction. Walter had been so impressed that he'd offered me a permanent job *and* a promotion after graduation should I wish to return to the NGO.

"Not that pet project, babe," Zara clarifies, excitement mounting in her voice.

"Are you telling me that Walter wants to run with KidStation?"

"No, I'm telling you he already did! Apparently, he's pitched it all over the place, and many agencies have been showing interest."

"Really!"

"Yep. And that's not all. Walter held off on accepting any offers because he was waiting for the big fish to start biting."

What feels like the first genuine smile of today splits my face. "And has a big company responded yet?"

"Not a big company, Tessa, the biggest! Two certified sharks have scooped it up. You're a genius, babe. And to think you only have three months before you've got to return to campus."

"Holy fuck, that's amazing! Don't worry, I'm only leaving for one last semester, then I'm back to be confirmed as the community outreach manager." It feels good to say, especially on a day like this one when I'm feeling out of my depth.

"Yeah, tell that to our director. He acts like you're about to divorce him and move to another planet, which is why he's sweetening you up. At this rate, he'll soon create the position of deputy director specifically for you, just so he can guarantee you'll come back to us after your graduation."

I laugh in spite of myself. "But I'll always be happy to write up proposals or take a look at anything he's got, even from school. He knows that."

"I'm sure he does. Anyway, for this project, you'll get to be the one running the show."

"Oh, wow, Zara, are you sure?" The scope of my second project is so wide, and I would have thought that Walter would split the duties more evenly with one, if not multiple, colleagues. "I really don't see myself achieving much within the three months I have left with Guardian Angels."

Zara makes a non-committal sound, and I imagine her shrugging. "I don't think it matters as long as you're there to kickstart it. And it's not just Walter, babe, everyone in the office wants you leading this project. I know because we took a sneaky vote behind your back."

"And?" I prompt, already suspecting what she'll say but wanting to hear the news.

"Duh! It was unanimous. You're doing this, Tessa, even though Walter hasn't said anything to you yet, as usual."

"Aww. Thanks, guys." It feels great to be seen as a valuable member to the team, like my contributions are not only acknowledged but also appreciated.

"Sure, babe. You deserve it."

"So, do you know who these potential 'sharks' are?" I'm already getting excited at the thought of leading my own project.

Zara pauses again, presumably to have another sip of coffee. "So, this is why I wasn't too sure about you coming back anytime soon. Now, we've got Boulder, a special needs academy in New York, and we also got the Fount in LA."

The smile wipes off my face as a chill runs down my spine. "The Fount?"

"Better believe it. The largest network of specialist oncology centers in the States."

It's owned by Nathan King.

Fuck.

I press my phone closer to my ear. "And did Betty have any idea which one Walter is leaning toward?"

With my rotten luck, I have a feeling it will be the latter.

"Of course we're flattered by Boulder's interest, blah blah blah, but come on, Tess, it's the fucking Fount! They have, like, the most advanced children's cancer centers in the country!"

I know. I fucking know.

"Betty says Walter is literally pissing himself with joy over this Fount deal. You're going to LA, baby! And I didn't even realize how close your Valencia is to LA. You'll get to see your dad anytime you want, too! Lucky you!"

Oh, hell no. I shudder in repulsion. "I can't do it."

"Sure you can," Zara coaxes, obviously mistaking my horror for modesty. "You'll be brilliant. To think an institution like the Fount doesn't already have what you're proposing says a lot about how awesome your ideas are, Tessa."

Zara's still talking on the other end of the phone, blissfully unaware of the terror spreading through my body.

"Walter is just giving you some space to spend time with your dad before telling you the good news. He's convinced that you'll be delighted." Zara pauses, then says, "Give me a sec, Tessa."

I hear shuffling in the background, during which time my mind has served me about a million reasons why this idea is an absolute disaster, so I no longer register when she comes back.

"Uh-huh, just as I thought. Betty is actually setting up a meeting with the Fount as we speak. I imagine Walter will see it fit to break the news to you a few days before the actual meeting, but consider this call a fair warning—and an early congratulations."

My heart is banging painfully in my chest. I would gladly run back to Detective Warner's office, grab the binder, and start reading those journals right now, if only to get me out of this situation.

I feel like a tiny bug caught in a giant spider's web.

A web I crafted with my own hands when I made that proposal and accepted the community outreach manager promotion.

"Thanks, Zara, you're the best." My voice sounds weak and thready to my own ears, but Zara doesn't seem to notice.

"Anytime, babe. Enjoy your time with your dad."

I'm going to be stuck in LA for three months. Working *with* Nathan King. An hour away from my dad and his shiny new fiancée.

This is a nightmare.

How will I face Nathan after what happened between us five years ago? I close my eyes in regret and mortification.

How did I even have the misfortune of crushing on a man like him in the first place?

It started in my sophomore year of high school. Things were rocky at home, and organizing charity events was my only escape.

I started the Children's Impact Club for sick children and that's how I met Nathan.

With mere weeks to our Christmas food drive, we'd run out of fundraising ideas, and I wasn't going to ask my dad.

Desperate for funding, I wrote to companies. Unlike others who just sent promises, the Fount Center sent a generous check, a tour invitation, and a meeting with their chief medical director.

I was sixteen, more into charity than boys, but meeting Nathan changed everything.

His blue gaze ignited a storm of butterflies in my stomach. My heart raced, palms sweated, and words escaped me whenever he spoke or simply gestured with his hands.

He was about the same age as my dad and very good-looking. But why my body was so hyper-aware of him was something I just couldn't wrap my head around at the time.

All I knew was he was just so... *there*.

Although I didn't fully get it, the feeling was one I enjoyed, a buzz I didn't get from anyone else.

So, I kept finding reasons to go back to the Fount Center and develop projects for their pediatric unit. And so, my passion for helping children caught fire.

It was much later, a year or two after our initial meeting, when my crush deepened into raging lust, that the details of what made him incredibly sexy hit me.

It was also when I realized that good-looking was too tame a description for Nathan King.

I just know I'm going to be a puddle of nerves the moment I lay eyes on him again because I bet Nathan remembers every detail of that night on the pier. He doesn't seem to be the kind of man who forgets anything.

Especially something as ludicrous as me giving him an unwanted lap dance in public.

Was it really unwanted, though?

There is one mostly-forgotten detail about that night, one I try my best not to think about for the sake of my own sanity.

Nathan was rock-hard and panting for me. He'd wanted me, for however brief the desire lasted.

I take in determined lungfuls of air.

Maybe there's a way I can play this situation to where I can go in, get the work done, and leave for Boston once again without any drama.

And *maybe* I could even get out with every ounce of dignity that Nathan's words stole from me five years ago.

Chapter Three

NATHAN

"Can you get pregnant at sixty-four?"

I look up from my desktop monitor, across my large, gleaming walnut desk and pin the one woman who means the world to me, with a shocked and mildly disgusted look. "Mom, come on—"

"Don't look at me like that, Nathan, I'm just asking for a friend," she says, or rather tries to say, with a straight face while polishing off the last of her buttered croissant.

"Of course you are." I snort.

She only shrugs, fluffing her glossy, dyed black curls, not bothering to deny the fact. "Are you done, darling?" She motions to my half-eaten breakfast and cooling coffee.

"Thanks." I nod, and she clears our leftovers, dumping them in the bin before returning to drop gracefully in her seat. She watches me expectantly while I appear to busy myself with the reports I'm leafing through.

I don't usually have breakfast, and she knows that, but I wasn't going to say no to her dropping in on me with food and conversation after almost a month of not seeing her.

She's been in Paris for the last month, launching her latest skin care product, and has only just returned yesterday.

Caitlin Murphy-King is the poster child for a person's physical looks not reflecting what they've been through.

She'd eloped at eighteen and married William King, a farmer. They'd sold everything to buy land in the citrus and grape belt of California, then settled in the small town closest to it: Valencia.

Unfortunately, their farm fell on hard times, and my father had to sell out to the Blackwells, a wealthy family filled with generations of farmers.

Tragedy struck again when my father died of bone cancer shortly after, leaving his young wife to fend for their toddlers by herself.

She worked two jobs during the day while enrolled in night school. Each day, her determination to succeed grew stronger. Now, she manages her own skincare and make-up line.

Ever since her new relationship began four months ago, sex, libido, and relationships are suddenly the only topics that she seems capable of discussing with me. Then, she inevitably ends up nagging me about my own relationship, or lack thereof.

"Nathan...pregnancy at sixty-four?" she pushes, clearly not taking the hint that I'm too busy for this.

I sigh. "It's not medically impossible, though highly unlikely. Why are you even thinking of that right now? And don't give me the whole 'asking for someone else' bull."

"Fine," she admits. "It's because I had a bit of a scare while in Paris. Nausea, bloating, achy breasts, the like. What was I supposed to think? And you know Lyle is insatiable, I mean, than man can—"

"Jesus, Mom, spare me the details!" My breakfast is already threatening to come back up.

Her familiar, musical laugh soothes me in a way only a mother's can. "I can't believe how prudish you can be sometimes, Nathan. You're supposed to be the expert here, explaining how these things work to the rest of us mortals."

"I deal with cancers, Mom, not doling out safe sex advice to randy seniors who are related to me," I say with bland seriousness.

She tries to look insulted, but the edges of her mouth twitch upward. "Can't blame me for trying though. At least one of us is thinking of carrying on the King lineage."

I don't even bother to respond, knowing that this line of conversation is a field of landmines. I simply return to the pathology reports on my desktop computer.

"I mean, anything is possible with hormones these days," she continues. "And like they say, if you want something done right, you should consider doing it yourself. Lyle's all in, too."

"Knock yourself out, Mom." I actually marvel at how she keeps finding new ways to spin the nagging-for-a-grandchild/find-a-wife conversation. She's nothing if not inventive, I'll give her that much.

"I mean it, Nathan. I feel like I could really do it. I only need the right doctor to help me."

She asked me three months ago to introduce her to one of my gynecologist friends just for a chat and check up, and I'd wondered why she needed it at the time since she had no worrying signs and kept up to date with her Pap smears.

Good thing I listened to my gut and declined, telling her to find one by herself. I'd hate to have to deck that friend of mine who helps my almost sixty-five-year-old mom to get pregnant again.

When I say nothing still, she continues, "And since you won't help me, I'll have to turn to Jackson. I know he'll find me a great gynecologist."

She's referring to my employee, the eccentric head of the remissions unit, and one of her favorite people in the world.

"You will do nothing of the sort, Mom," I warn.

She rolls her blue eyes in mock frustration. "Fine, I'll ask someone else, but just know that I'm serious."

I look at her, letting her know that I don't believe her ruse. I know her true goal is for me to be the one who has a child, but I'm just not ready for that step right now.

To be honest, I'm not sure if I ever will be, but no matter how many times I try to tell her that, she doesn't seem to understand.

I've found that it's better to just let her play her games. "I can see that you are, Mom, which is why I wouldn't dream of getting in your way."

"Anyway," she huffs, changing the subject. "How's the crew here? Everyone okay?" She's referring to the tight-knit staff who work at the Fount.

Hospitals can get depressing, but my staff more than make up for it by operating like one big family, both in LA and across our other centers in the country.

Of course there's rivalry, and small feuds are never in short supply as with any family, but I feel very lucky to be heading such amazing people.

"We're doing awesome, Mom. We win more than we lose."

The thousands of dollars that go into preaching prevention and screening on TV and social media is money well-spent.

It ensures that people come get checked out earlier and the disease is caught when the options aren't as limited.

"You know, Nath, your father would be proud of the man you've become," she says while a wistful smile crosses her lips.

"Thanks, Mom, that means a lot."

"Of course. In any case, it's been great seeing you. I need to run, I have a meeting in"—she checks her Rolex—"half an hour."

"So, are we doing dinner at my place next month or yours?" I ask.

We're both usually so busy that unless we deliberately plan to have dinner together once a month, we could go months without seeing each other.

As she rises up from her seat and collects her things, she sends me her classic, narrow-eyed "mom" stare. "Yours, Nathan. And Lyle is coming, too."

"Sure, no worries. You know I like the guy, I'm just not too keen on seeing his tongue down your throat during dinner." I stand to see her out, my hand going around her slim shoulders.

"I'll try and behave this time." She laughs, and I know it's not a promise.

"And I'll try and remember to have a bag handy so I can throw up in it." I smile in return.

Just before she leaves, she turns back to say, "Nathan, I kept thinking about it while in Paris. You should get aggressive advertising for the project you told me about. It's an amazing idea."

She'd been with me last month when I first received the proposal from Guardian Angels Network. I'd been unable to contain my excitement about such a genius concept and immediately told her about it.

"I agree, it's brilliant. I'm already working with a team who will sort out all the logistics."

An image of Tess Blackwell appears in my mind, and my chest squeezes tight.

She's always been a gorgeous girl, but the Tess I saw last week was fucking karma. If I had to draw my dirtiest fantasy, it would be her.

Sexy, confident, and smart as hell. I know she recognized me with the flicker of emotion I caught in her gaze the moment we were introduced. But she'd continued her pitch without another glance at me.

"That's wonderful, Nathan. Be sure to keep me posted."

"Will do." I bend to kiss her cheeks at the door. "Love you, Mom."

"I'll give Lyle a nice kiss for you," she teases.

"Whatever." I smile in spite of myself. I'm happy that she's found love again, but hell, she's my mother. It's always going to feel a bit strange watching her gush over her man like a teenage girl.

And speaking of teenage girls...

Tess, the girl who used to hang on to my every word, has turned into an industrious and capable woman.

A woman who, to my utmost shock, got me harder than I remember ever being, forever eradicating my ability to think of her as innocent.

And given my reaction to seeing her again last week, she'd better run.

I wonder what that bastard John Blackwell will do if he ever finds out that his daughter will be promoting his worst rival.

One who rose from working on one of his family's orchards to owning ninety percent of those orchards now.

A fact that is most likely lost on Tess. Otherwise, why would she come to the Fount? To me?

Or perhaps she knows and just doesn't care.

Chapter Four

NATHAN

I planned this meeting with her one week ago, and I've geared myself up for her arrival as best as I could, even telling my assistant to give me a heads-up when she's on her way to my office.

Still, nothing prepares me for the sight of her again.

She's beyond gorgeous. Honey blonde hair, tamed into a neat bun at her nape, big, green eyes that are darker and more muted than they were five years ago, and a mouth that could draw even the most devout man into wondering what it would be like to crush his lips to hers.

Seeing her for the first time in five years last week was like being hit by a freight train. My only saving grace was that I was one of many observers in the room.

As the chief medical director, my presence wasn't necessary at that meeting, but Rafe Alvarez, my new head of pediatrics, asked for my help in ironing out the details of our collaboration with the Guardian Angels Network on the KidStation project.

The NGO director, Walter Heche, brought the KidStation team to the meeting.

Imagine my shock upon realizing that the head of that team would be none other than Tessa Blackwell.

The girl who subtly inserted herself under my thick, unfeeling skin.

The one who, in the twinkle of an eye, turned into an irresistibly sexy woman, tailor-made to obliterate my common sense with her words alone.

The moment she entered the conference room, I was physically unable to look away from her for more than two seconds at a time.

Good thing she did a lot of the talking so I had an excuse to keep looking at her.

She was magnificent.

Even as a teenager, Tess had the uncanny skill of getting my attention.

The first thing that caught me was her distinct cursive handwriting in the compelling letter she wrote me while in high school.

I'd been immediately curious to meet the writer. I mean, I didn't know any adults who could write so beautifully, let alone a teenager.

So, I'd had my assistant write her back, inviting the entire impact team to sit down with me.

Then, I saw Tessa Blackwell in person. A shy but outstanding sixteen-year-old with expressive green eyes and a quick wit.

One who was unfortunate enough to be adopted by the one couple on earth I cannot stand.

But, I recognized and nurtured her interest in studying medicine.

In time, I also saw her struggle with grief when she suddenly lost her mother.

And then, finally, to my shock, I became the object of her desire five years ago.

I often prided myself in how controlled I am. But that night, I was hers to control.

And as she moved sinuously against me, a shocking thought smashed through my defenses like a sledgehammer.

Tessa Blackwell is mine.

More than anything, I'd wanted to put my mark on her. To have her writhing beneath me as I pounded her into a screaming orgasm and spurted my essence deep inside her.

For twenty years, my ambition has been to convert every Blackwell triumph into a King conquest.

And now, Tess Blackwell, the forbidden fruit of my long-standing rivalry with John Blackwell, is being offered to me by Walter Heche on a platter of gold.

Fate truly has a flair for the dramatic.

Except that last week's meeting was like watching a live performance of indifference. Tess barely glanced my way.

I hated it.

So, in a mix of exasperation and curiosity, I asked for a meeting with the head of KidStation – Tess herself. Walter Heche, practically tripped over himself to set it up, overjoyed to have the CMD personally invested in the project.

The brief flash of irritation on Tess's face before she composed herself was all I needed to see.

And now there she stands, in my office, dressed in a soft, silk shirt tucked into a short, black skirt that lovingly accentuates the curves of that made-for-sin body.

"Welcome," I say, leaning back in my swivel chair and gesturing for her to sit opposite me in front of my desk.

She doesn't make eye contact, and her lips are tight when she says, "Thanks, Dr. King."

Nathan. I want to correct her, but I stop myself. "I was surprised to see you on the project last week, you know."

She narrows her eyes for a fraction of a second. The expression is gone in an instant, her face falling into a mask of indifference.

"Well, it was my proposal, and I happen to be managing this campaign on behalf of the Guardian Angels Network."

"I thought you were studying medicine at UCLA."

Her gaze finally meets mine, and I see the emotions in her expressive eyes. Distrust and hurt. Something squeezes in my chest.

Tess used to look at me with open trust, and perhaps a bit of awe, and I didn't know how much it meant to me until just now– being the center of attention of those green eyes that could probably solve quantum physics on a coffee break.

"I guess I found medicine too restrictive. Not to mention, boring."

I know she's not referring to the course, and a part of me wants to smile at her innuendo, proud of her sass.

The other part yearns to persuade her just how fun I can really be.

Instead of doing either, I just nod in understanding. "That's a shame. You seemed really interested in a career in pediatrics."

She shrugs nonchalantly and the action draws my attention to her breasts.

I snap my eyes back up to meet hers, but apparently not fast enough because the glint in their clear green depths tell me that she caught my wandering gaze.

Get it together man.

Tess continues speaking as though nothing happened. "I still love children. I just found a better way to help them and a way that I'm much more passionate about."

I hear her say the word "passionate," and immediately, my cock twitches.

Passionate was the way she dug her nails into my thighs and moaned my name.

Of course, my eyes have to find the perfectly manicured fingers she has intertwined on top of the desk.

And imagine them wrapped around my cock.

Fuck.

I promised myself I was not going to let my long-neglected libido run the show. I really should have gotten laid after I saw her last week.

Although something tells me it wouldn't have made any difference.

I force myself to focus back on the conversation. "I have to agree that you're very good at non-profit management, Tess. The Children's Impact campaign you ran in high school is still one of the best there's been for decades."

I should know. I attended the same high school, and I'm still a member on the school board.

She says nothing, so I continue speaking. "So, was there a reason why you chose a five-year co-op program instead of a straightforward three or four-year degree?"

For a moment, I think that she won't answer, but finally, she shrugs again, and this time, I manage to keep my gaze trained on her face.

A soft look enters her eyes. "It was less expensive that way."

I wait for her to elaborate, trying to mask my surprise. The Blackwells come from money. The last few generations have not been as prudent with resources as their predecessors, so their wealth has steadily declined over the decades.

John, the sole surviving heir, has somehow managed to hang on to the last two orchards, much to my annoyance.

He should still have enough money to put his daughter through college. Unless the jerk didn't set anything aside for her, that is.

Again, she doesn't say more, so I push. "What about your father, Tess?"

Her eyes harden. "My dad and I don't see eye-to-eye on a great number of things, and we're not on speaking terms. Not since my mom died, anyway. To change colleges and move to another city, I was going to need a lot of money, so it made sense to go for the cheaper option."

I know I just heard the short version. She would have needed more than just money. She most likely had to take a gap year or two, transfer her credits from UCLA, whip up a kickass application, apply for financial aid, and possibly work herself sore to achieve all that.

And she'd done it for the last five years.

Tess Blackwell might look like she just walked out a man's dirtiest fantasy, but under all that sex appeal is a spine of steel. "I'm proud of you."

"Thank you." She says, only it sounds a lot more like *"Fuck you."*

She's angry. *Still? After all this time?*

"So, tell me about your proposal, Tess." I want to keep her talking and get behind the professional front she's trying so hard to maintain.

"Walter already did. And so did I in the detailed onboarding email I sent out."

"Yes, I'm aware, but I want to hear you tell it."

Her nostrils flare, the mask starting to slip off her face. But she takes a deep breath, expertly sliding it back on.

"Okay, imagine kids living with cancers and long-term illnesses. Now imagine them in a vibrant world where they're no longer on the sidelines but right at the heart of it all," Tess explains, her eyes lighting up with every word.

She pauses for a breath, and I lean in, captivated, signaling her to continue.

"In this world, they can dive into their school work, lose themselves in fun games, and forge friendships. Think about it, even a chance at a first crush, with, of course, parental consent. It's just the tip of the iceberg, really. The possibilities are endless."

"It's not just a platform; it's a lifeline, a game-changer," I say, genuinely impressed.

A subtle smile flickers on her lips, a clear sign of her dedication. She's not just in this job; she lives it.

"So, when are you available to start?" I ask, eager but wanting to align with her timeline.

Walter Heche hinted they could start right away, but I'm curious about Tess's personal timeline. I'm ready to offer any flexibility she needs.

"We're set to hit the ground running," she says with a spark of determination. "We plan to immerse ourselves in the pediatric wards and clinics this month."

"Sounds great. Thank you, Tess." She isn't just planning a project. She's orchestrating a revolution for these kids.

She looks up at me. "Well, I figure the sooner we kick things off, the sooner I can be out of here."

Wow.

That statement grates on my nerves like a discordant note when, in fact, it should be music to my ears.

Tess, undeniably stunning, will be a distraction. My work is too important and I can't afford to let anything, not even someone as compelling as her, sidetrack me.

So it's best she starts ASAP and leaves quickly.

Before the less rational part of me escapes its tightly held confines and takes charge.

"In that case," I say, "Rafe—Dr. Alvarez—will work with you to map out what your team needs and create a schedule that works for everyone."

"Alright, Dr. King."

"Nathan, please." This time, the words roll out before I can stop them.

I tell myself it's only because she's known me for ten years, not because I'm dying to hear my name on her lips again.

Surely, my mind must have conjured up the intense pleasure I felt the last time it happened.

She only nods tightly, and I see from the stubborn jut of her lovely chin that she has zero intention of calling me that.

I huff out a breath.

Christ, this woman is pushing buttons I hadn't even realized I had. Her indifference is messing with my head.

I refuse to cope with her cold mask one second longer. I want to see the playful twinkle in her eyes and the dimpled smile that puts even the prickliest person at ease.

I'm going to crush this wall of ice, right fucking now. "Tell me something, Tess. Why did you even leave California in the first place?"

Her eyes snap to mine, bright with fury.

That question hit a nerve.

"Rich of you to ask me that since you ran me out of town."

Good, we're getting somewhere.

"I would have believed that was true, especially with you leaving UCLA for Boston except that I checked your resume last week. You'd already been in the Boston co-op program when you returned to Valencia."

"So?" she murmurs testily.

"So, you'd already left, anyway. I didn't run you out, as you say. I suppose the better question is, why did you come back to Valencia all the way from Boston if you weren't speaking to your dad at that point? Somehow, I can't believe it was for the Annual Citrus Fest."

The fact that she evades my question makes me wonder if it had anything to do with something that has been niggling in my head since last week.

Did she come back to see me?

She'd looked worried when she'd come up to me right after my speech, but we kept getting interrupted.

And then, she came back to me that evening and showed me that my resistance was, indeed, as brittle as glass.

Something keeps telling me that she came all the way down from Boston to see me that night.

Conceited much? My sensible brain hisses at my leaping heart.

"You were needlessly callous that night," Tess says instead, as if she knows I'm thinking about that night.

True. The night I rejected her is still imprinted in my memory. Casual sex isn't something I do.

I've spent the last two decades with the singular focus on obliterating my enemies and expanding my own empire to the exclusion of almost everything else.

Apart from friends I can fuck *and* talk business with, I don't have the time or inclination to meet women.

But the moment she moaned my name that night, I was horrified at the sheer willpower I'd needed to summon to restrain myself from tearing off her clothes and rutting her into the weathered wooden planks of the pier.

Because although she's a Blackwell, she's also Mary's daughter. Adopted daughter, but still. I should have been repulsed. Instead, I'd been furiously turned on to the point that she'd noticed.

Thinking of Mary Blackwell makes my fingers curl into fists now, the way they always do every time I remember what happened all those years ago.

Tess most likely has no idea I know much more about her family than I let on. That I could never stand her mother and that her father hates me.

Right now, she watches me, expecting an answer. So, I give her the only one that makes sense.

"I spoke to you that way because someone had to yank you out of your downward spiral."

Her eyes flash with anger. "I wasn't going down any spiral."

"You were, Tess," I say gently. "You've never liked the town, but you bent over backward trying to get it to like you."

I used the word town as a euphemism for father because I'm not sure how much of the hard truth she's ready to accept.

The last time I talked about her mother, she didn't take it well so I can only imagine what she would do if I were to mention her troubled relationship with her only surviving family member.

Her nostrils flare. "I was doing no such thing."

"You held on to that rejection and tried using sex to numb the pain. Wasn't it after you learned not to care and left everything behind that your life started to really take off?"

"You're *wrong*." Her voice is thick with emotion, and her cheeks redden with anger, or maybe embarrassment? Perhaps it's both.

"Which part is wrong? That you *weren't* trying to get me to have sex with you to get over the pain or that things haven't improved for you since you stopped looking back?"

"I wasn't."

I cock my head in doubt.

"What *were* you doing, then?"

She crosses her arms, distracting me again as her cleavage becomes more prominent.

She needs to stop doing that.

You need to stop looking, perv, she's dressed modestly.

Again, she notices the direction of my gaze. This time, she doesn't ignore my blatant stare.

She looks down at herself, then deliberately lets her eyes rise slowly back up to me in a way that feels like a hot tongue caressing my naked skin.

Fuck. Don't do that, Tess.

The eyes that finally creep up to meet mine are half-lidded and sultry.

Exactly the way she looked that night by the lake.

I know even before she speaks that the temptress is back, and she's about to say something obscene, so I steel myself.

"I came on to you because I was horny and I wanted you to fuck me, Dr. King. You know, that urge *adults* get from time to time without needing to be psychoanalyzed? I certainly didn't need you to give me a dickish sermon or act like my father."

Christ, her mouth is lethal.

Speaking of fathers, I state the obvious, but not because I think she's missed the fact. On the contrary, something tells me that particular kink turns her on.

"I *was* your father's age, you know. I still am."

She shrugs. "That didn't stop you from getting hard for me, though."

Okay. This conversation is *not* going the way I thought it might when I started it.

I admit that I may have triggered the derailment when I started pushing her to talk, but Tess has taken charge and is now leading us down a dangerous path.

Because I'm rock-hard and throbbing, and the little speech I gave in my head about staying focused now sounds like the ramblings of a lunatic.

"That was only a natural reaction any man would have to a lapdance, Tess," I reply, still striving for composure.

"And what about right now, Dr. King?" She purrs, "What's your excuse?"

Christ. I'm done fighting this. If that's how she wants to play it, let's fucking go.

Not bothering to deny what she's saying, I stand and round the table toward her. "I have no excuse whatsoever."

I see her eyes widen as I approach. I don't crowd her, though. I only lean my butt against the desk while looking down at her.

She stares at the bulge in my pants, then looks up at me questioningly.

Holding my palm out to her, I wait until she puts her delicate hand in mine to say, "You are driving me crazy, Tess, and you know it."

Relieved that she hasn't resisted me, I gently pull her to her feet and toward me until she stands in between my spread thighs, about a foot away from my body.

"Come here," I urge, daring her to close the gap between us.

She doesn't obey. Instead, she takes a couple of steps back.

Her gaze falls to my crotch again, and she slowly, deliberately licks her full, pink lips. In response, my cock jerks behind my suddenly too-tight pants.

I'm pretty sure she saw that, too.

"Dr. King, sorry to disappoint you, but I'm not interested in any of that." She gives me another slow once-over. "I'm here to work. Nothing else. So, I suggest you try harder to keep your hands to yourself."

She manages to sound both scathing and seductive, making it hard to think straight as images of bending her over my desk and fucking her into submission begin playing over and over in my head.

"Duly noted, Ms. Blackwell." She means to torture me. I can take it.

Hopefully.

My sexual restraint is legendary. I've even been called a monk by friends and close employees.

Before Tess sat on my lap five years ago, I'd not had sex in well over six months.

But this forbidden woman brings up a much different set of emotions within me. She breaks every ounce of control I have without even trying.

She says my name, and lust clouds my vision.

I know I'm not going to last three months with her. Not if she keeps looking at me like she wants to devour me while telling me to fuck off.

Hell, I'll be lucky to last three weeks.

Still, challenge accepted.

I shake the hand still in mine and shoot her a grin, which probably looks predatory, but I don't care at this point.

Tess just showed me how she likes to play. And fuck if I don't love it.

"Welcome to the Fount." *Baby girl.*

Chapter Five

TESSA

FOUR WEEKS LATER

The Guardian Angels team meeting with the software developers for KidStation takes longer than expected, and we've overrun our allotted time.

If I had known it would take this long to go over everything, I would have pushed the meeting to later in the week.

"Guys, I'm afraid we'll have to adjourn until another day." I check the time. "We should have been out of here two minutes ago and we don't want to keep the next users waiting."

Because everyone seems to want to schedule their clinics and meetings earlier in the week, and leave the rest of the grit work like ward rounds and major surgery lists until later in the week, the conference rooms are always fully booked on a Monday like this one.

I'd often wondered if it wouldn't make more sense to spread out these meetings throughout the week so that the demand for conference rooms wasn't so heavy on Mondays.

I even suggested it to some of the unit heads, but the answer was always the same from every one of them and confusing as hell.

Bottom line is, nobody wants to not have meetings on a Monday. Yep, it's one of those Fount things.

Which means it's *The Hunger Games* for conference rooms on Mondays, and everyone would rather play it than move meetings to another day.

There's so much to discover here – the quirks, characters, and its unique rhythm. It's like a whole new ecosystem.

I thought Guardian Angels Network was my fit, but I'm swiftly getting drawn to this team of incredible people under Nathan King.

We don't see very much of him because he has so many commitments in different places across the States and internationally. But we still feel him in the very pores of the Fount.

Tim, one of my assistants who has a clear view of the corridor, cranes his neck back to peer through the glass walls. "Actually, I can confirm that the three o' clock guys are already here. And," he adds, his pitch rising with excitement "oh shit, it's the King himself, with a few of his princes to boot!"

My stomach twists into knots.

"Really? The chief medical director has a meeting here with his residents at three and we haven't been booted out on our asses yet?" Diane, my second assistant, also twists around to see.

"Okay," I start gathering up my things, grateful to have something to occupy my suddenly shaky hands. "We really should leave now. How about we reconvene sometime on Thursday or Friday? Does that work for everyone?"

"You mean we shouldn't wait till next week Monday?" Diane snickers, and if I wasn't so nervous, I would join her.

Instead, I shake my head firmly. "Too bad we have a deadline to crush, we can't be indulging in any dystopian custom. So Thursday everyone?"

There's general assent, so I continue, "Okay, I'll have the desk clerk look at all our schedules and book a convenient time for everyone on Thursday."

I pack up quickly, wishing the room had a backdoor I could slip through.

Why are you running from him? My inner voice mocks me.

I can't even lie to myself. It's because I know that my stupid crush on Nathan King is back in full-force, and since I haven't seen him in almost a month, I don't trust myself not to do something silly.

Like ogle him in front of everyone.

I've hardly even seen the man, but the way other doctors, nurses, and patients talk about him like he's their best friend has somehow unearthed all those feelings I thought were buried away.

Hearing everyone else's experiences with him reminded me of the times I would email him about charity events I was planning. And despite how busy he was he'd always make time to respond.

Since I can't very well disappear from the room, I wait until the rest of my team piles out, then I follow.

He's having a discussion with Tim when I step onto the wide corridor, so I pick up my pace, hoping to leave before he notices me.

Despite myself, my gaze is helplessly drawn to his profile. He's tall, his shoulders and biceps filling out the tailored white shirt in a way that should be outlawed. His thick, wavy hair is slightly tousled, and his ever-present five o'clock shadow adorns his chiseled jawline.

So. Fucking. Hot.

My greedy eyes beg to linger on him but I give myself a mental shake. As I try to walk past the group Kaiden, one of the residents, stops me.

"Hey, Tessa! Just the woman I've been trying to find." He leaves the group heading into the conference room and jogs back toward me.

Seeing no way around having to stop and talk to him, I muster a smile when he reaches me. "Hi, Kaiden, you doing alright?"

"I'm good, thanks, just gearing up for in-training exams. You know how it is." He replies, his smile is warm, but there's a hint of something more in his dark gaze, a subtle flicker of interest.

I nod, thinking of Isa's similar grind as a surgical resident. "No doubt you'll nail it Kaiden," I say with a confidence I hope he finds reassuring.

"Thanks, Tessa." He shifts slightly, an eager note in his voice. "Actually, I wanted to ask you something. We're throwing a little get-together for Jackson and Gary's anniversary. It'd be great if you could come."

"Oh, that sounds nice. I'd love to." Getting invited to such a personal event proves that the Fount lacks the cliquish mentality I've heard about in other hospitals, where there's a strict hierarchy and doctors think themselves above everyone else. "When is it?"

He winces slightly. "This weekend. Yeah, it's short notice..."

"Shoot, I wish I could but I've got an event this weekend too. It's an engagement party."

Kaiden's smile doesn't falter. "Really! That's probably going to be more fun than we'll be having."

Barely stopping myself from cringing, I shake my head, then shrug. "Not really my scene, but we'll see how it goes."

Just then, out of the corner of my eye, I catch Tim slipping away, and Nathan approaches us.

Shit.

"Demetrius." Nathan's deep baritone echoes on the almost empty corridor, and we both look up. As it's customary among attendings, Nathan calls Kaiden by his last name.

With only a stern look and a jerk of his head toward the conference room, Nathan wordlessly orders him to join the rest. "Tell the others to give me five, and you're free to start without me."

"Sure, Dr. King. Tessa." Kaiden reaches out to squeeze my elbow, then does as Nathan asked, heading into the conference room.

Nathan stops in front of me while I clutch the bundle of papers I'm holding in front of me like a protective shield.

"Tess." His smile is friendly, but his eyes are anything but that. They're searing, sending tingles of awareness down my spine.

I school my features into polite indifference. "Dr. King," I reply.

"I've been terribly busy, or I would have been in touch to see how you're getting on. I trust everyone has been looking after you?"

"Oh, yes, everyone has been really nice. I need to only ask, and they're all eager to help in any way they can."

"I'm glad to hear that you're liking it here."

I nod, but neither one of us has anything left to say.

It occurs to me after about a full minute that we're standing silently, staring at each other. I quickly look around to see if we're being observed and see Kaiden and a few others openly staring at us.

Geez. Why does there have to be glass everywhere? No privacy!

"Um, they're waiting for you... for your meeting." I nod toward the conference room.

Nathan gives a cursory glance over his shoulder, but in that split second, the scene inside has transformed.

Before, everyone was gawking like meerkats spotting a low-flying plane, but now they're all laser-focused on Kaiden, who's taken center stage at the table.

If I wasn't so high-strung, I'd find it comical how quickly they'd switched from wide-eyed rubbernecking to intense concentration, like a bunch of kids snapping to attention when the teacher walks in.

"It's just a revision chat before they take in-training exams, and that group is pretty much set to ace them already," Nathan informs me, a proud look on his face.

That's not what I'm worried about. I'm more concerned about what they'd say about us.

I couldn't cope with the looks I would get and how word would spread around the hospital.

Nathan's voice cuts through my musings. "So, you mind me asking where you're going this weekend, Tess?"

Surprised that he overheard my discussion with Kaiden when he was deep in his own, I debate not telling him the truth, but in the end, I decide to come clean.

"My dad's engagement party."

A furrow appears between his brows. "And why on earth would you do that?"

I know he's remembering the day I'd told him about overhearing my dad tell Mom what a waste it was to have adopted me.

I shrug. "Because he invited me."

I've resolved to give my dad one last chance to mend things, beginning with attending his engagement party. However, I'm not sure I should share this with Nathan.

"Okay." He says the word like he's waiting for a better reason than the one I just gave, like there's an unsaid "and" at the end of his sentence.

"I mean, it's been five years, and I'm here in LA. Plus, Joyce, his fiancée, seems like a nice person. Besides, I'm a big girl. I'll be okay."

With my hesitant tone and refusal to make eye contact with him, I'm not sure if it's Nathan or myself that I'm trying to convince.

Nathan only watches me, his eyes full of things that he wants to say, but I know he won't voice them.

"Alright," he concedes, then changes the subject. "By the way, if you or the Guardian Angels feel like you need to reach me and I'm not around, you can speak to Doug Harris. He's my personal assistant."

"Okay, thanks, Dr. King," I say with a bright smile.

His wince is concealed, but I catch it still.

And because he doesn't seem to be in a hurry to leave, despite the glances we're getting from the conference room, I say, "I should head out now. I don't want to keep you any more than I already have. I'll, uh, see you later."

I walk away quickly, feeling the weight of Nathan's gaze on my back the whole time.

Chapter Six

TESSA

How many fake smiles can I force until my teeth splinter out of my mouth?

"I can't tell you how glad I am that you made it, Tessa."

I force yet another grin at Joyce. She's actually the least insufferable part of the evening, which is surprising for me, seeing that she's marring my dad. But she seems nicer than all of my dad's ex-girlfriends combined.

For one, she's made the effort to know my name. Then, there's the fact that she's blissfully unaware, or has chosen to ignore, the fact that I don't speak to my dad and I had zero plans of attending just a few weeks ago. She obviously doesn't do drama.

But since being in LA for the last month, been asking myself why I still want to reconnect with the only family I have left, even if it is with someone as hateful as my dad.

Because having a messed up family has got to be better than the feeling of being absolutely alone in the world.

Detective Warner has been in touch a couple of times, but I've managed to stall him, saying that nothing in the binder rings a bell. They haven't found any new leads yet, either.

"I'm glad to be here." It's a lie, but Joyce beams at my words.

I feel discomfort burn within me as I look around. The expansive hall is decked out in full glamor, with colors of white and gold on every conceivable surface. It looks quite expensive, and I wonder lazily how my dad's paying for it.

Over the past decade, his businesses have been taking financial hit after hit, and the orchards are gradually being sold off. The remaining two orchards, while being the largest, are more for storage, preservation, and product testing than actual farming.

Not that my dad cares that much, given that he has never readjusted his spending behavior to fit his dwindling resources.

Joyce most likely is paying for everything.

Smart choice. At least then my dad won't be able to hold anything over her head.

I look around at the people milling about, who seem only capable of staring at me. Only one or two return my smile. They are the usual suspects, older men and women who witnessed the majority of my parents' marriage, yet concocted the most senseless rumors.

Like the one that the reason their marriage finally crashed and burned was because of me.

Because despite my parents' belief that having a preteen daughter would suddenly solve all their marital problems, my presence wasn't the miraculous cure they were hoping for.

But seeing as I was immensely grateful to be adopted, I worked like hell to get my parents to like each other and me.

By the time I was old enough to know better, the damage was already done.

You had one job, Tessa, to make your mother happy, and you couldn't even pull that off...

My dad's terse voice floats in my head. Unexpectedly, tears spring to my eyes, and the room feels too small.

"Excuse me, I need to get some air," I say to Joyce, who has started looking at me with concern. Before she can reply, I turn around, grab a flute from a passing waiter, and walk toward the French doors.

The balcony overlooks an expansive, well-kept lawn with hedges of flowers arranged to form a maze. It's dark outside, but thankfully, it's also silent and empty. Most people are inside the hall. I put my champagne on the concrete ledge looking down into the garden.

It was stupid, really, coming here. Working with Nathan in the past month had given me the false sense of having got over what happened to Mom.

I wanted to prove myself, and mostly to Nathan admittedly, that I was no longer the broken woman who couldn't face her past.

It feels like that's all I've been doing. Proving a point to Nathan, even though something I see in his eyes tells me that I don't need to.

Since that first day in his office, he's not bothered to, or rather, he's been unable to hide the fact that he wants me. It's in the way he looks at me, and I feel it clear across the room, even when other people are around.

And from what I hear about him from people who've worked with him for over a decade, he's practically a monk.

He doesn't look or *feel* like one, though. He looks like six foot three inches of pure sin.

And I've been pretending I'm indifferent to him, acting distant and aloof.

"Tessa!" I flinch as I hear the booming voice of my dad, and I steel myself as I turn toward him.

He looks older, slightly paunchier with his cheeks red with excitement, or wine, or both. His arms are open wide, and there's a grin plastered on his face. His eyes, though, are as cold as ever.

I fight to stay rooted to the spot as he approaches me, and my discomfort piles up as he folds me into his arms.

"What are you doing here, Tessa?" he whispers through his false grin.

"Why, Dad, the same reason you're hugging me like you love me. Optics. Nobody should know you haven't laid eyes on your beloved daughter in five years."

He holds me at arms length, his grin still firmly in place, looking at me the way a father might gaze at the daughter he's missed dearly.

"You decided to leave and cut all contact after your mother died. Did you really expect me to chase you around the damned country?"

"No, not really. It hurts that you didn't try, though." More than I care to admit.

Maybe that's why it was that much easier to leave after Mom's death. As quiet and unassuming as she was, she was the glue that held us together.

"I have better things to do than to lose sleep over a headstrong, ungrateful child."

I suck in a breath. "You've always known how to make a girl feel special, Dad."

Sometimes, I imagine I'd be better off if John hadn't adopted me. Maybe someone else who wanted a child for the right reasons would have come for me.

But then, I might not have met Nathan or discovered my passion for helping children or my skill in managing charities.

"I know this isn't the time or place to talk about this," I begin, knowing that this interaction is likely the only chance I'll get to speak to him. "But, Dad, did the police contact you about Mom's journals?"

My dad's smile half-vanishes, and I can tell he's barely hanging onto the last threads of his doting father act. "So, that's why you came back? You believe all that bullshit?"

"The police certainly think it's worth reopening the case for."

"Tessa, you know there's no point in rehashing the past. She's long dead. Leave it be."

"Have you even seen the entries? Did you know that she kept journals?"

The look on his face is a mix of alarm, regret, and irritation. Because I spent a good chunk of my life studying this man's expressions, I know exactly what it means.

No, he had no clue she kept journals. He sorely regrets the fact that he never knew this fact, despite being married to her for twenty years. And no, he has not yet seen those journals. Most likely because he's been evading the detectives.

"Neither of us knew why she wrote those things. Maybe there's more to her death than what we know. She certainly seemed like she knew it was coming." I say.

His smile is now completely gone, replaced by an ugly sneer. "I know you want to hold on to the past, but trust me. Your mother was a devious and deranged actress. There's a whole lot of facts you don't know. I saw through her act from the start, but you have always been gullible to deception, despite my best attempts to make you streetwise."

I step back from his embrace, a chill running down my spine. I know my parents weren't happy together, but hearing him talk about her with such vitriol makes me wonder if he ever loved her at all.

Why, then, would they even marry in the first place?

"Even if you're right and she's all of that and worse, Mom's not here anymore. If she had something to say before she died, don't you think we owe it to her to hear her out? We're supposed to be her family, right?"

His mouth twists into a snarl. "Sure, whatever. But maybe get on with it after my wedding? I'm getting married in a few weeks, and I don't want whatever the fuck else you think you've found out about your crazy mom blowing up the town and causing a ruckus."

I feel like he just suckerpunched me. Laying my palm on my suddenly hurting stomach, I stare at him, barely believing what he just said. But, before I can even formulate a reply, a cold, clear voice rings out from behind me.

"Easy there, Blackwell. She was the woman you married at all costs, after all."

I whirl around. My heart skips a beat when I see Nathan, dressed immaculately in a dark gray suit, stepping toward us on the balcony. He's beyond gorgeous, filling out that custom-made suit in a way that makes my mouth go dry.

But he's not even looking at me. His eyes are trained on my dad.

And he looks thundcrous.

"King." Dad's voice is icy, losing the last, faint traces of friendliness. "Surprised to see you here."

Nathan comes to stand behind and slightly to the side of me, a bristling, solid presence.

He doesn't have to touch or even look at me, but he might as well have put an arm around my waist and dragged me into his chest with his defensive body language. Anyone from a mile off can see that he's protecting me.

"One of the hazards of inviting people you don't want to see, Blackwell, is that you run the risk of them showing up."

"A mere courtesy. It's not like you deign to grace anything in Valencia with your precious presence, except for the damned Citrus Fest."

Nathan just stares at my dad like he'd like to wring his neck. My heart skips another beat, this time in fear.

My dad jams both hands deep into his pockets. "And now that you're here, albeit unwelcome, perhaps you could refrain from butting in on family conversations that don't concern you?"

Nathan lifts a brow. "I should think it concerns me, remotely at least. We're talking about Mary and her *black* heart, are we not?"

My dad's face pales, then goes blotchy with rage.

Looking from one seething face to another, I become more confused by the minute. I know my dad doesn't like Nathan, but I'm surprised to see that the feeling is mutual. In fact, it seems as if Nathan hates him more. And why are they speaking in what sounds like code?

My gaze still flitting back and forth from those two, I see Nathan's face darkening, even as the corner of his mouth lifts in a mocking smirk.

And I see the wheels turning in my dad's head as his hands, now out of his pockets, curl and into fists. Then he levels me with a look of revulsion.

It's obvious that he thinks I'm with Nathan. I'm still trying to figure out what the deal is between these two, so I can't even bring myself to care what he thinks at this point.

After seconds of the silent stare off, where I half-expect for fists to start flying, my dad mutters, "Screw this shit," and stalks off, returning to the party inside.

What the hell just happened?

I turn to Nathan, intent on asking him that question. But before I can even form the words, he grabs my hand. "Let's get the fuck out of here."

Not waiting for my response, he pulls me back inside, past the tittering throng of people around the dance floor, and heads for the exit. I go willingly, still numb from my unpleasant exchange with my dad and what I just witnessed.

Chapter Seven

TESSA

Nathan leads me toward a waiting black limousine. Still not saying a word, I let him settle me inside of it. Within minutes, we're speeding away from the banquet hall and the watchful eyes of the party guests and my dad's rage and disgust.

I look back at the venue, which is now a spot of light in the rear windshield, still unable to believe that Nathan came to the party at all. Not only did he come, it looks like it was for the singular purpose of getting me out.

The idea that he might have done that for me makes my belly flutter. The shock of my dad's cruel words ebbs away, replaced by the novelty of being alone with Nathan.

He sits beside me, a silent yet comforting presence, but he seems lost in thought. His jaw is tight, and he's staring out of the window.

Something is eating him up.

He yanks off his bowtie and undoes the top two buttons of his shirt, then sprawls back against the seat, his large frame taking up most of the space in the car.

I become more aware of him as his drugging scent fills my nose. It's still the same from five years ago. Earthy and masculine.

I decide that conversation will be the best cure for this mounting desire to just sit and inhale the guy.

LA is about an hour away from Valencia. Plenty of time to get high on him and do something really stupid, like bury my nose in his neck.

"Where are we going, Dr. King?"

He winces, pausing for a beat before responding, "I'm taking you home, Tess. Unless you'd like to go elsewhere?"

Elsewhere, like your place? I crush that wild thought.

"No, home is fine. Thanks." My home is one of the apartments in the Fount's massive six-storey staff quarters. My team and I were delighted to be offered free accommodation as part of the package we negotiated.

"You didn't tell me that you were coming here, too," I say into the growing silence.

A muscle jumps in his jaw. "I wasn't going to attend."

"So, why did you change your mind?"

He finally pins me with a fierce look. "Why do you think, Tess?"

"For me?"

"To get you *away* from there, yes," he clarifies.

Tilting my head to the side, I look him over like he's a puzzle I'm trying to solve. "But when I told you that I was coming here on Monday, you didn't ask me not to come."

At the very least, he could have warned me if he foresaw me having issues with my father, but then again, I probably would have just blown him off.

Nathan must know where my mind is at because he shoots me a deadpan stare and cocks his eyebrow. "Would you have listened if I had?"

He has a point there.

"So, you were friends with my mom?" I ask, needing to make sense of the mutual hate between him and my dad.

"What gave you that idea?" Nathan questions instead of answering me.

"Because when you said her name, you said it with…"

What? Familiarity? Passion? I'm not sure. "Like you knew her," I finish.

Nathan turns to face me fully, his gaze skimming my face for a few seconds. Finally, he says, "We went to high school together, along with your *darling* father."

My brows furrow. He's not exactly answering the question of whether he and my mother were friends or not, but it's obvious that there's no love lost between him and my dad.

"You and my father seem to hate each other. Does it have anything to do with my mom, Dr. King?"

Nathan winces again.

"It probably has more to do with me buying back a certain piece of land from him and refusing to stop there. I want the rest. Everything he owns. So, I keep making him offers that he can't to refuse."

I note that he's evaded my question about my mom, but what he's revealed is equally intriguing, which only begs the question of what would make Nathan want to do that to the Blackwell empire.

"Why did you want those lands, Dr. King? You're one of the most successful doctors in the States, not to mention the busiest. You hardly have time to farm."

This time, he doesn't bother answering my question; instead, he whispers gruffly, "Tess, do you know that in a whole month, scratch that, in five years, you haven't once said my name? Not since that night."

Oh, shit. I know where this conversation is heading.

I've felt an inexorable pull to Nathan all month but have fought against it. Hard.

His crazy schedule has made it easy on me to do so, too. Apart from the day in his office where I couldn't resist playing with him a little because I saw how he struggled to keep his eyes off me, I've avoided him.

But right here in this confined space, with nowhere to hide and a determined man aiming to destroy my composure, my resolve to avoid him might hold as firm as wax before a naked flame.

"Nathan," I begin, hoping to pacify him by giving him what he wants. Perhaps he won't try to wear me down if I use my professional tone. "Look, I'm sorry if I misled you—"

"Fuck. Say my name again," he gruffly commands.

My skin tingles, and my nipples tighten at his raw, needy tone. This battle may already have been lost before it even began. How am I supposed to resist him when he talks like *that?*

"Nathan," I whisper.

"Come here," he growls, dragging me closer, then practically dumps me onto his lap. I brace my hands on his shoulder and chest to keep myself from crashing into him,

He's so big and warm, and I feel surrounded by him. I'm still fighting the urge to stroke the unyielding muscles beneath my hands when he suddenly grabs my hips and pulls me flush against his hard length.

"Nathan!"

"Feel what the sound of my name on your lips does to me."

I moisten my lips nervously, and like a beacon, his gaze drops to my mouth.

He's going to kiss me. Oh, God. Nathan King is about to kiss me.

And then, his large hand is cupping my jaw as his mouth slowly descends on mine.

For a moment or two, I'm too shocked to respond. I'd been imagining how it would feel to kiss him for ten years, and now, out of the blue, it's happening.

He starts off with a small peck, then another, as if testing how we fit. Then, he goes to town.

His lips move unhurriedly over mine, teasing and coaxing. He nibbles and sucks on my bottom lip, then very gently grazes it with his teeth in a way that drives me mad. He does the same thing to my top lip.

What he's doing feels like art. Like he's exploring the shape and texture of my mouth. I've never been kissed like this. My lips go slack under his, inviting him to play with me more. He changes the angle, then deepens the kiss, sweeping his tongue inside my mouth. As soon as his taste hits me, I begin to crave more.

When I start to return his kisses, he draws back, luring me to follow him and forcing me to declare without words how much I want him to keep going.

Enjoying his taste too much to stop, my hand goes to his stubbled jaw and spears into his silky hair to stop his retreat and pull him back to me.

All teasing gone now, the kiss turns ravenous, a decadent melding of lips and tongues and moans I'm unsure who's making. I feel his cock twitching under my butt, and I can't resist grinding back against him.

I'm so busy drowning in his kisses that I don't recall rearranging myself to straddle his thighs. Next thing I know is that I'm shaking, so close to orgasm from having been grinding my clit against his hardness.

Suddenly, he breaks the kiss, puts a hand on my hip to stop my writhing, then looks straight into my eyes. "Tell me why you went to the party, Tess?"

I already gave him a few reasons yesterday. That he's asking me again, right here and now, means that he didn't believe me.

I consider what to tell him this time to get him to drop it. Did he really have to pick now to bring it up again? I mean, really, right now that I'm seconds away from coming?

"The truth," he rasps, somehow knowing that I was about to come up with another excuse.

"I-I wanted to see him." There's a pause where he says nothing, simply raising a single eyebrow.

I miss having a family. I bow my head because I'm too ashamed to say that part out loud, but I suspect that Nathan already knows.

I hazard a look at his face, expecting to see disgust at my weakness, considering what he said to me five years ago, but the admiration I see in his eyes has me squirming. At least, that's what I think his look means.

Before he can question me further and steal more secrets from me, I reciprocate with one of my own.

"So, what do you know about my…?"

"Father? He's not much of one from what I've seen over the years."

I actually meant to say my mom, but ouch.

His words shouldn't hurt, but they do. My breath leaves me on a deep sigh, drawing Nathan's attention to my hard nipples poking through my tight, green, strappy dress. I'd decided to forgo wearing a bra under the thick bodycon material.

When he looks back up at me, his eyes are almost completely black with only a thin ring of blue.

It's such a turn on to see the depth of his desire.

While it wouldn't be the worst thing in the world to lose myself in Nathan's arms tonight, to let him wash away the bitter taste of tonight's events, I'm *also* reminded of that night five years ago. The one where Nathan had humiliated me, even when he had a full-on erection.

He could very well be planning a repeat performance now.

"So, is this the part where you give me a scolding again for going to a place where no one gives a shit about me?" I whisper.

"No, Tess. This is the part where I tell you that you're fucking stunning."

I suppress a shiver. I had a master plan all figured out, one where I put Nathan through the paces by remaining formal and aloof. One compliment shouldn't melt me into a gooey puddle, but my body can't help responding to his words.

Still, I can't let him see how much his adoration makes me want to give him everything he wants tonight.

So, I smirk, meeting his gaze. "I know that."

I know he likes my answer when a predatory smile crosses his lips. His fingers run down my spine and keep moving, all the way down my hips and my ass, and he starts rocking me against his hardness.

"Do you, now? Go on, show me." He reclines against the backrest... relaxed and expectant. As though we've done this many times before.

His dominance is a huge turn-on for me, and the way he moves me against him, unerringly hitting my clit with the perfect amount of pressure makes me want to give up all control and just do whatever he says. To let him do whatever he wants to me.

I bite my lip in excitement as I slowly lower the straps of my dress, exposing my full breasts to his hungry gaze.

"Fuck, Theresa."

The lust I see in his gaze makes my core pulse with need, and I feel another surge of wetness slip through my folds.

He's barely even touched me, and I'm already this far gone.

And then, his fingertips stroke the soft globes of my breasts but avoid the tight, aching peaks, even when I arch my back, inviting him to do as he likes.

Before long, I'm panting, unable to bear the torture any longer. I want his hands on my nipples more than I want my next breath, so I beg. "Nathan, please, touch me."

"You're so beautiful when you beg. But you'll go first. Take my cock out," he orders in a gruff voice that instantly makes the remaining vestiges of my failed plan to act unaffected by him disappear into oblivion.

I obey without thinking, my hands trembling with desire as I undo the top button of his tailored pants and pull down the zipper.

He lifts his hips up slightly to let me pull down his pants and briefs, and then, his cock falls hot and hard against his belly.

Oh, my God.

I gasp. He's huge. Long and veiny, curving to a point that I bet goes way past his belly button.

As if sensing my intimidation, he puts his hand around my jaw and lifts my flushed face to his. "My turn," he rasps.

His other hand goes to the apex of my thighs to drag the drenched crotch of my panties aside. Then, still holding my gaze, he very slowly inserts a thick finger into my core, wrenching a ragged moan from deep within me.

"So fucking drenched. You feel beautiful hugging my finger, Tess."

My whole body trembles as my eyelids flutter closed. I'm fighting to keep still and not eagerly fuck myself on that finger that's gliding in and out of me.

"So, tell me, baby," he says conversationally as he finger fucks me, "how long have you wanted me to touch you like this?"

My eyes fly open. Is he asking how long I've had a crush on him? "Nathan—"

"How long have you wanted my cock? Touched yourself here wishing that it was me instead?"

"I-I—" My face and chest go beet-red, and I'm grateful that it's dark. I could say five years, but I'm too amped up to sell the lie. He would see right through my act, anyway. I decide that it's better not to say anything at all.

His thumb presses against my clit, and I tremble as he strums the swollen nub until my mouth goes slack and my moans get louder. Then, he stops. That gets my attention.

When I open my eyes, I see that he's watching me, still waiting for an answer.

"When, Tessa? Since the night of the Citrus Fest?"

I shake my head. Might as well be honest since the faster I respond, the faster he'll get back to touching me. "Before then."

He starts moving his fingers again.

He's really good with his hands. Like he knows exactly where and how to touch me. Maybe because he's a doctor?

And then, I can't think anymore as he presses against a spot that makes my breath seize. Goosebumps cover my entire body, and I let out another moan as the pleasure floods through me, numbing my brain. I forget to feel self-conscious this time as the words pour out of me.

"It was way back since high school. Since the first day I saw you," I whisper in a cracked voice.

His quick gasp could signify surprise or disbelief. Or both.

He freezes.

"Don't stop," I moan, needing more friction against the tightening knot in my core, but instead of giving me what I need, he takes his hand away from me.

My lids fly open, and just when I'm about to demand to know what his game is, I find him watching me, his expression a mix of desire and... horror.

A part of me always wondered if, all the while, he had some idea how hard I was crushing on him. I see now that he really had no clue.

Oh shit. Is he... freaking out?

Somehow, his reaction to my revelation makes me crave him more. My gaze locks on to his. "Nathan, *please*" I whimper, "I need you."

I think I'd die if he decides to stop now. *Or kill him if he tried to.*

After what seems like ages, which could have been mere seconds, his initial shock dissipates, leaving only lust etched on his features. He slowly captures one of my hands and drags it down to wrap it around his straining cock. "It's all yours. Take it and fuck yourself with it."

His words ignite a fire that burns away all the shame I felt just now. I scramble up to my knees, tuck the head of his cock against my folds, then push down about an inch.

His size makes me gasp, and my first instinct is to rear back. But he doesn't let me. He holds me still, hugging me against him as he rains open-mouthed kisses against my neck and collarbone.

"Easy there, Tess."

He continues kissing a path down to my breast until he takes a taut nipple in his mouth and sucks strongly. I gasp and arch to give him more.

His hand cups my other breast, his thumb and index finger tugging on my nipple and ending with gentle pinches that makes my pussy clench against him, greedily seeking more of his invading girth. I push down another inch and moan.

"Too big for you?" he murmurs silkily.

Yes, it is.

Not wanting to risk him stopping, I shake my head in a frantic no.

I want him so bad, I'm delirious with the need to have him fuck that relentless, achy knot inside me that makes me want to scream.

"Good. So, you'll take all of me like the naughty girl you are, then."

He wraps a strong arm around my waist, then slams me down onto his cock.

"Ah, God! Nathan!" I scream. Realizing too late that his chauffeur is probably getting an earful, I shove my face into his neck to muffle the sounds coming out of me.

The stretch, the tightening, the bite of pain, and the mind-blowing pleasure make me jerk and writhe against him, even though he's holding himself very still inside me.

"You okay?"

I only moan in response.

"Go on then. Make yourself come."

"I c-can't." I'm a trembling mess, and my knees already feel like jelly. "You do it, Nathan. Fuck me hard," I whine in a voice I hardly recognize.

And even though I'm barely going to be able to walk tomorrow, I know it'll be so good that I'll thank myself for letting him do this to me.

"Bossy, little thing, aren't you?" He smacks my ass, triggering another clench of my pussy against him as a gasp bursts from me.

I've never been spanked before and I can't work out why it hurt but also sent a jolt of pleasure straight to my core. I immediately want him to repeat it.

As if reading my mind, he spanks me again. And again, carrying on until I'm moaning and grinding against his cock. My ass feels hot and tingly, and I'm riding on the cusp of orgasm.

Oh fuck, I won't be able to walk *or sit* tomorrow.

How does he know *exactly* what to do to drive me insane?

He grabs my tender ass and lifts me slightly up, then he starts to rock upwards into me, slowly at first, then picking up his pace as I get even more slippery.

And then, he's slamming up into me, maneuvering me in a way that grinds my swollen clit against his pelvis. All the while, I'm crying out his name, begging him to keep going.

He does. Until I'm gasping, and my core is rippling with the insane amount of pleasure that is spreading outwards onto my skin, which already feels like a hundred feathers are running against it. He doesn't even stop to let me catch my breath.

My orgasm doesn't take long to hit, ridding me of thought, of awareness of my being. Of everything except the man who is filling me like he was made for me.

Nathan holds me firmly and fucks me through my orgasm and straight into another one. All I can do is hold on for dear life—and scream like a banshee.

When his breath gets choppier and his thrusts get faster and shallower, I know he's going to come. "Tessa," he growls, trying to lift me off him.

I tighten my arms and thighs against him, not wanting to let go of that delicious girth for a single second. I want everything Nathan has to give.

"No, I want it all, Nathan." I'm all but sobbing with desire.

With a loud, pained grunt, he shudders, then spills himself into me. My walls contract around him, as I feel his cock spurting in release. I close my eyes against the intense wave of euphoria, unable to stop trembling like a leaf.

Finally, my breathing slows, so I drag in a deep breath. And another.

This—*he's* too much. Who the hell called this man a monk? He's a sex fiend. Nathan King knows exactly what he's doing in the sack.

"I should have done this ages ago," he says around a grunt, his fingers slipping themselves around my neck as he pumps into me a final time.

I whimper in response, unable to think beyond the fact that sex has never felt this way before. Ever.

It must be that my brain has recognized Nathan as the one I've been fantasizing about for over a decade, so it amplified the sensations a hundredfold because, fuck.

And as Nathan's arms enclose around me as I struggle to regain control of my trembling body, one thing stands out clearly in my head.

How will I keep saying no to him?

Chapter Eight

NATHAN

I made one of my life's biggest goofs. I fucked the wrong woman, even though it felt incredible doing it.

That impending sense of doom clings tightly to me as I walk into my once-a-month remissions clinic.

Jackson Ames, a specialist oncology nurse and head of the remissions unit, is in the large assessment room, bent over a patient and copying her vitals signs into an iPad while deep in conversation with her.

Jackson runs a weekly clinic to see the regulars, those who have beaten the disease and have remained in remission for years while I do a monthly clinic, also on a Monday, for those newly cured of cancer.

Jackson straightens the moment I enter.

"Morning, Dr. King!" he calls.

"Jackson. Ms. Sileby," I respond, twisting my mouth into a semblance of a smile. "Feeling good?"

"Top of the world," Pat Sileby, a sixty-six-year-old survivor of melanoma, beams. "Only, Jackson here is tormenting me for losing a couple of pounds, but I've told him that it's intentional, so I'm good. Tell him, Doc."

I know better than to get involved in Jackson's business, so I just smile. "Sure, I will."

"It's not a few, Pat, it's twelve whole pounds," Jackson gripes. "I'm not having your BMI fall, just so you can pour yourself into a bridesmaid dress."

"It's a mother-of-the-groom dress, so that shows how much you know," Pat returns.

He crosses his arms across his chest, narrowing his eyes at her playfully. "I know this much: lose one more pound, and I'm scheduling you an appointment with our dietician for further review."

Pat's mouth snaps shut, and she huffs, sufficiently chastised, while Jackson smirks in triumph.

All my patients have a healthy revulsion for the Fount dietician. Her results are pure magic, but she manages to come up with the vilest tasting smoothies and concoctions.

I don't have to start my own clinic for another fifteen minutes, but I head across the corridor and into my consulting room.

Usually, I would stay and chat with a few more of Jackson's patients, many of whom I haven't seen for years, but today, I'm as tense as a cat on a hot tin roof.

I collapse into the plush leather seat, then blow out a calming breath.

I've been out of town all week, and all the while I kept telling myself that it was the distance affecting me, that I would settle once I got in today, but I can already see that won't be the case.

I hold a hand out in front of me and see the faint tremors in my fingers.

I'm the furthest thing from settled. I'm fucked, is what I am.

Where the hell is Tess? My mind screams at me. *Get her!*

It's been a week since John Blackwell's engagement party. Since the limo. Since Tess blew the top of my head to smithereens.

After Tess stopped trembling, she simply whispered a shy "thank you" before kissing the spot on my neck that she'd been worrying with her teeth while coming on my cock. She disentangled her limbs from mine, then sat next to me, putting her head on my shoulder.

And then, she promptly dozed off.

I couldn't have made up a more perfect solution for avoiding the awkward aftermath of sex in a car if I tried. I should have been jumping for joy.

Instead, it galled me because it was obvious that Tess didn't see what happened as more than an outlet for the night's difficult emotions.

She even fucking thanked me.

But I can't complain about it since we'd both used each other to feel better.

Hearing John's comments about Mary had triggered my deeply conflicted feelings toward the woman. I resent her almost as much as I feel sorry for her.

Because that woman took my brother from me.

Still, I couldn't help jumping to her defense because that's what Ciaran would have done. Walking into a conversation where Mary was being shredded to pieces, a reminder that John never loved her yet was too cruel and selfish to let someone else love her, it triggered an unbearable ache inside me. It left me wanting to hit someone.

Or fuck someone.

And Tess was there. A woman who'd been driving me crazy with lust, and one I know for a fact also uses sex as therapy when she's hurting badly. She just also happens to be John Blackwell's daughter.

There couldn't be a more perfect cure and retribution all rolled into one if fate itself had conjured up the scenario.

The only problem is this damn withdrawal syndrome I have from her. I took one hit, and now I'm hooked. One week and I'm literally shaking like an addict craving his next high.

I'd left LA the morning after the party for a week-long working trip, delivering lectures and honoring speaking engagements in various teaching hospitals across the country.

I hate traveling, so I prefer to schedule my trips around the same time, so I can complete them in a few large chunks. For a whole week, it seemed like every other thought I had was about Tessa.

With difficulty, I drag my focus from my raging hormones and power through my clinic. Thankfully, there's no bad news to deliver, as all my patients have stayed in remission.

By noon, I'm as cranky as a bear with a sore head. I really thought my longing for her was because I'd been so far away.

Apparently, I'm clueless about how these things work because little did I know that being in the same building as Tess and not seeing her would be a far worse torture.

"Dr. King?" Jackson is surprised to see me leaving as I walk out of the consulting room.

"What?" I almost feel bad for snapping at him. I usually pride myself on being a personable boss, but today, I can't muster up the self-control to keep my temper in check.

"Nothing, we still have a few walk-ins this afternoon."

Closing my eyes and cursing myself for my one-track mind, I race to find a solution that works for everyone. It only takes me a second to find one. "Give them my apologies and see them yourself, will you? I have somewhere to be right now."

The Guardian Angels' office.

Jackson is delighted at the opportunity I've just given him. And I know he's more than capable, too.

Because I know that it's still ultimately my responsibility and that I'm scheduled to run the clinics until three o'clock, I turn back to him just as I'm stepping out of the glass double doors. "If anything needs my attention, page me."

"Sure thing! Thanks." Then, as if just remembering something, he calls out, "Dr. King, the remissions team is having a bit of a get-together next week, and this time, we'd really like you to attend."

Geez, this is what, the fourth party this year? "Check with Doug. If I'm not otherwise engaged, I'll have to think about it."

That is, if I'm not attending another patient's funeral or playing mediator for another internal disagreement or doing a million other tasks. All these take precedence over letting myself indulge in something like a party, however enjoyable it might be.

As CMD and lead oncologist, I'm the captain of a ship with three crews of sailors who don't always see eye-to-eye.

The dying, palliative, or "pals," crew are those with terminal cancers who I have to issue weeks, sometimes days to live.

The living, remission, or "rems," crew are those who are lucky to have beaten the deadly disease. And boy, do they live the heck of life.

The last chunk of patients I work with are those for whom the dial could turn either way, otherwise known as the treatment crew. Usually admitted for surgery, chemo, or radiation, these patients are either hope or angst-filled.

Sometimes, tempers run a bit high when one crew thinks that another is getting special treatment for their patients, like the parties that the rems crew likes to throw.

I take the elevator to the floor that houses the Guardian Angels Network offices, but when I see the mocking, red OUT beside Tess's name on the digital status board, a ball of irritation settles in my gut.

"Hi, Dr. King." Tess's assistant, Diane, comes over to me when she sees me. "Did you want Tessa?"

Funny way to put it. I incline my head and smile wryly despite my frustration. "I see she's not in today."

"She's moved things around so she can have Monday afternoons off. Most clinics are on Mondays, but the bulk of surgeries and chemo appointments happen later in the week."

When I furrow my brows in confusion, Diane explains further, "Patients tend to attend clinics alone but will have friends and relatives with them when coming for surgeries or chemo. Tessa wants us to focus on getting as many patients and relatives to sign up for KidsStation beta testing as possible."

"I see. That makes sense. Thanks, Diane."

I'm about to leave when Diane adds, "She should be with the kids now."

"What kids?"

"The ones in Unit F."

The isolation ward. A wave of panic hits me. Tess should not be going there, least of all by herself. There are stringent rules and regulations everyone must follow if they want access to the ward, and by going by herself, she wouldn't know any of the dos and don'ts.

"Thanks, Diane." I return to the ground floor, then step outside the building.

It's starting to rain, but I don't bother to change course and take the overhead walkway connecting the Fount buildings because that would take too much time.

I don't bother to look for an umbrella, either. I simply stride across the stone paths of the Fount complex until I reach the opposite building where the other wards are.

I'm drenched by the time I get to the isolation floor, but it doesn't matter since I'll have to change into scrubs, anyway.

The children here have compromised immune systems, so staff have to be very careful about spreading any germs to them.

"Hello, Dr. King," the nurse in charge greets me. "Dr. Alvarez didn't mention you were dropping by this week."

I grunt. "It's fine, Marta, I'm not doing a round. Is Tess—I mean, Ms. Blackwell—here?"

Seeming to comprehend the issue after taking a second to think about it, she looks guilty and has the grace to blush. "Dr. King—"

"How long have you been letting her do this?"

Her mouth tries to form words, but it takes a minute for her to compose herself enough to explain. "I'm sorry, it's because infection control approved her two weeks ago after she completed her training."

"I see."

Of course, one swish of her ponytail and these guys would give her anything she wants. At least they had the presence of mind to put her through training first, so that knowledge alleviates some of my worries.

"Do you want me to get her for you?" the nurse asks.

I wave a hand to dismiss the question. "Never mind, I'll find her."

I turn on my heels, leaving a surprised, somewhat pleased looking Marta behind, and stalk to the changing room, peeling off my damp clothes so I can change into dark blue scrubs, then I push through the double doors leading into the isolation ward.

Two of the four walls of the wards are made of glass, transparent so that the nurses can easily observe patients. The blinds are open, so I can see inside the rooms. I know which one Tess is in, because there's only been one child in admission here this week.

Skylar, an eleven-year-old kid with lymphoma, sits in a lotus fashion on her bed, chattering away, her face lit up with excitement. Tessa sits at the foot of her bed listening raptly.

I should go in and get her out. She shouldn't be here. To be fair, however, she's following protocol because she's in scrubs, gloved, and masked, and her hair is up in a neat bun.

I push the glass door, and it opens silently.

"... don't think I'm pretty."

I stop at the sound of Skylar's voice. Skylar started her treatment a year ago, but she's now nearing the end of her chemo cycles.

She's winning the battle, although her immune system has taken a big hit and her hair has yet to to grow back.

"Why would you say that?" Tessa asks. Her back is turned to me. I can't see her face, but I drink in as much of her as I can from this angle.

Much of her skin is covered, but the parts I can see make my palms itch to touch her. Her blonde hair, now in a prim bun, just reminds me of how it spilled down her back that night in the limo.

Would she like her hair pulled while I fucked her from behind? Something tells me that she'd like almost anything as long as I was deep inside of her.

Aren't you being a bit cocky there, caveman?

Except that I can't help it.

My thrill of excitement makes it almost impossible to focus on Skylar's next words.

"It's taking forever to grow back," she mutters. Tessa's frame blocks a chunk of the girl's face, but I can see her sunken eyes go hollow with sadness. "And Nurse Marta says that it might not even look like it did before when it does come back in."

Tess points her hand to the girl's chest. "Well, you know, as long as you're pretty in there where it really counts, it doesn't matter what color or texture your hair is. Or even that you have hair at all."

"But how would you know?" Skylar's eyes are filled with awe as she looks up at Tessa. "You've got a ton of hair."

"Well, when I was eleven," Tessa says, her voice low, conspiratorial, "someone at the orphanage shaved off my hair while I was sleeping."

Skylar's eyes widen, and she gasps. "No way!"

Tess nods solemnly.

"But why would they do that?"

Tess shrugs, releasing a small laugh as she seems to remember that time in her life. "To be mean. I didn't want to go to school, and I tried to wear a hat, but it wasn't allowed."

"So what happened?" Skylar leans forward in anticipation, and I find myself just as eager to hear the rest of it.

"It took a little bit for me to adjust because people needed time to get used to the new me, but at the end of the school term, guess what?"

"What?"

"I ended up being more popular. They thought I was super brave. I even got a secret admirer."

"Really?"

"Yes, I had freshly picked flowers put on my desk every week for a whole year."

Skylar gasps.

"Plus, I had my Christmas wish granted. I got adopted." The reluctant smile that had stretched my lips dies.

Fuck. Her parents never deserved her.

"Oh, Tess, that's great." The girl bounces on her tucked haunches, and she gifts Tess with a beautiful, genuine smile.

"Yes, so you see, you don't need hair to be loved. And I think you're the prettiest girl I've ever seen, with or without hair."

Skylar's grin lights up her face.

I squint at Tessa, more impressed than surprised. I've never even seen her interact with a child before. I know she's always had an interest in children, but seeing her passion, kindness, and maturity does something to me.

I step into view, and Skylar looks up and greets me with a small wave. Tess turns to look at me, and I notice how her shoulders stiffen the moment she sees me. I'm not sure whether to be gratified or pissed off by that.

"How's Supergirl Skylar today?" I move closer to the pair.

"I'm good. Look, Dr. King, Tessa came to see me." She gestures, holding her arm out to Tessa.

"I see that. It was very nice of her, wasn't it?" I smile, even though Skylar can't see it behind my face mask.

"Oh, she's the best," Skylar heartily agrees, bouncing on her haunches again.

"Tess?" I call when an awkward silence overtakes the room.

"I was just leaving, Dr. King." Tessa stands and straightens the edge of the bedsheet.

"Promise you'll come back soon," Skylar says, the moment she notices Tessa starting to leave. The young girl's eyes are anxious and desperate, like she's afraid that she'll never see Tess again and she's mourning the woman's absence already.

It's obvious that Skylar is already attached to her.

Great.

"Of course," Tess promises, following me out the door after I say my own goodbyes.

I lead her out of the ward, pulling off my face mask as I lead her further down the corridor, to a spot where we're partially obstructed from the view of the nursing station by a wall.

I turn and simply look at her—what parts of her face I can see, anyway. I've been dying to see her again, but now that I'm in front of her, I'm not sure what to say.

Tessa beats me to it. "She's lonely. Marta says that no one has been in to see her for two days."

"Nor will there be for the next couple of weeks."

Tessa's eyes go wide with surprise. "What? Why?"

"Her mom lives two hours away and has four other children, all under age seven. You know how kids that age are with germs.

Skylar is pulling through, but the chemo knocks out her immune system. She's going to be fine, though. It's her final cycle."

"Oh, I see." A frown appears between her brows, and I yearn to erase it.

"But," I continue in a softer tone, "I've arranged to have two girls her age and similar clinical state transferred from Glendale, so they can hang out, do pillow fights, shave off each others' hair, and whatever else you girls do at that age."

She laughs. "You're kidding!"

"No, they arrive in a couple of days. It's meant to be a surprise for Skylar, so I haven't told her yet," I warn.

"Oh, my God, my lips are sealed. But how on Earth did you pull that off? I didn't know you could do that."

"Yes, it's possible with a lot of logistics and by calling in some favors. Getting the parents involved can be tricky, too. So, you see why your project would really help my kids, and my soon-to-become arthritic knees, if I no longer have to continue to grovel every time we get a patient with long admission into F," I finish with a wry smile.

"Nathan…" Her eyes go soft. I've never given her a gift before, but something tells me I just did. "You're…that's wonderful. I didn't think you'd…" she trails off.

"Didn't think I'd what?" I need to see the whole of her face, so I reach out and take her mask off. Ah, yes, those soft pink lips I'd like nothing more than to sink my teeth into.

Because I want to keep touching her face, I tuck a loose tendril of hair behind her ear. When that isn't still enough, I linger, running my finger along the shell of her ear. Then, I get even greedier and wrap my hand around her jaw.

I know it's only a matter of seconds before I take her mouth.

She probably knows it too because she steps back, looking around. "Nathan, someone might see us and talk."

I move closer. "No, they won't."

She looks at me like I've lost my marbles. "Workplace gossip? Could anything be more sensational than that?"

"Why, the dreaded Valencia grapevine, of course." I chuckle when she moves away again. This time, the wall stops her. "I'd think having been bred on that you'd have thicker skin by now, Tess."

I take another step toward her, closing the distance she's put between us.

"Besides," I whisper, bending to kiss a spot on her exposed clavicle, then trailing soft kisses up her neck, slowly making my way to her sexy mouth while a low moan escapes her. "There's so much bad news around here, we're too busy trying to cling to whatever slice of happiness we can find."

Finally reaching my goal, I press a chaste kiss on the corner of her mouth before fitting my lips over hers, gratified when her mouth immediately opens and her tongue darts out to meet mine.

Chapter Nine

NATHAN

THE KISS GOES ON and on.

The way she responds tells me that she missed me every bit as much as I did her. As her fingers run through my hair and tug on a few locks, lust clouds my mind, and without thinking, I grab handfuls of her ass and cradle her against my hard length.

Apparently, I'm not the only one who's suddenly taken leave of their senses because Tess responds by hooking a leg around my thigh and opening her core fully to me. She starts to rock herself against my thrusting pelvis as her moans get louder.

Then, as if suddenly realizing where we are and how close I am to dragging her into the changing room and relieving us both of the tensions of the past week, she freezes and jerks away from me. I let her go, even though that's the last thing I want to do.

"Nathan." She pants, putting a hand on my chest and pushing me ever so slightly.

I take a step back. "What, baby?"

"We can't—" She swallows and looks away. "Um, we shouldn't... and about the other night...we need to talk about it."

"Here we go," I mutter, already knowing what she's going to say. "Okay, I'm all ears. But not here. You can tell me over lunch." At least then I'll have a greater chance of changing her mind.

She looks like she's about to argue.

"It'll just be at the cafeteria on this floor. We won't even need to change. Come on." I take her hand.

"That's kind of what I wanted to talk about. I'm not sure being seen together is a good idea. You're the CMD."

"Well, I'm a doctor first."

"Yes, but you're not just a coworker. You're the boss."

I huff out a breath. "Tessa, unless I pin you up against that wall like I did just now, this," I say while pointing back and forth between us, "us talking, having lunch together, is considered normal territory around here."

She cocks a skeptical eyebrow.

"Relax, baby. We've just seen a patient together, and we're off to debrief."

"Ri-ight, and do you call all your female colleagues and workers 'baby?'"

The jealousy I hear lurking in her tone causes me to fight off a smirk. "Only the ones named Tessa."

Before she can argue further, I lead her down to the cafeteria and find us a table in the corner.

The server comes over to take our order as soon as she sees me, but otherwise, the cafeteria is empty, a fact that makes Tess relax.

Our order arrives in a flash, and I watch her dig into her sandwich with gusto, her lids fluttering at that initial taste.

Why does everything about this woman have to be so damn sensual?

To get my mind out of the slope it's merrily sliding on, I do something I never do with women I want to fuck. Small talk.

It's guaranteed to bore me to tears and effectively kill my boner. Every time.

"So, are you doing anything interesting this week?" I begin.

"Oh, yeah. I've been drafted into the remissions unit's party planning, and by default, Tim and Diane are also pitching in." She's practically bouncing in her seat, and seeing her so excited makes me smile.

"You like to plan parties?"

"I'm good at planning stuff, generally. Food drives, fundraisers, and the like. I haven't done a party before, but I figure it can't be much different."

She leans closer as if revealing a secret. "Besides, I think Jackson is doing most of the planning. He just really enjoys getting people together and giving them orders."

I chuckle. "That he does."

He's about five two, but he might as well be seven feet tall with his reach and influence in my hospital.

Tessa's excitement fades somewhat as she scans me with a curious look. "They say you never attend, though. Why?"

I snort. "The rems unit throws parties every five seconds. I'm often too busy to attend."

"But the patients love them! And these parties have given the hospital a lot of publicity and visibility. They essentially make you richer and more famous, Dr. King." Tess cocks an eyebrow in challenge.

"I know, and I would never get in their way. But the treatment and palliative teams can get sensitive about these parties."

An incredulous expression overtakes her face, and I can tell how nonsensical she finds it to be.

"Are they for real? Surely, they know that the thousands of dollars raised in these events go to funding palliative care and active cancer treatments, don't they?

"Of course they know." I shrug. "But it doesn't change how they feel."

She shakes her head. "Hmm, so that's the reason you don't attend. But whose side are you really on?"

"None, I'm neutral," I lie.

"Ha! Come on, you can admit it." She gives me a conspiratorial wink. "I know how you like to appear stuffy and proper, but underneath it all..." she trails off, biting her lip.

"What?"

"Underneath, you're a savage, Nathan."

Blood rushes to my cock with an alarming speed, even as the corner of my mouth lifts in a smirk.

You have no idea, baby.

"You love the parties, don't you?" she presses, and there's a flirty tone hidden in her voice.

Watching her relax and tease me lightens the mood between us considerably, and I'm suddenly having more fun than I've had in years.

"I suppose when you look at it objectively, the parties do more good than harm," I say with a poker face.

"I knew it!" She chortles gleefully.

I surprise myself by asking, "Do you want me to come to this one, Tess?"

A hopeful smile paints her luscious lips. "Really! You'd attend?"

"If you want me to, I'd consider it."

She taps a finger to her chin, pretending to mull it over. "I dunno. Depends on if you're going to wear a suit and look like a stuffy CMD?"

"You bet I am."

"Killjoy," she teases. "I was hoping we'd get to see those bulging muscles in a tight T-shirt and jeans."

"Bulging muscles, huh?" I cock an eyebrow, unable to hide my smug smile.

She doesn't say anything, but her eyes trace my arms, as if she can already picture me wearing such an outfit in her head.

Then, shaking her head as if to dispel the images, she says, "But then again, we don't want you hogging all the attention. The patients are the guests of honor, and the rest of us should blend in, not steal the show."

I'd come shirtless if it would steal your attention all night.

"So you're coming? I won't tell anyone, so no pressure. You can always change your mind later if something changes," she coaxes.

Her thoughtfulness tugs at me. "Okay, Tess, I'll be there."

"Yay," she cheers and fist pumps.

Her joy makes me laugh. And arouses me to no end. I didn't think it was possible to feel both emotions at the same time, but when it comes to her, I realize that everything I thought I knew is no longer true.

Unable to wait anymore, I circle back to the reason I brought her here in the first place. "So, about the other night?"

She bites her full lower lip, and I know that she's remembering the graphic details.

Good.

"Tess, I know you're not about to tell me you regret what we did in the backseat of that limo."

"Nathan..."

I shake my head and wave my hand to cut off her protests. "You fucking loved it, Tess. You came so hard on my cock that you dropped off to sleep right after."

She flushes scarlet, but I feel zero remorse for my bluntness.

"And snored quite loudly, I might add."

"I did not snore!" she protests. As if suddenly finding the bun too tight, she yanks out the hair tie and fluffs out her blonde waves.

I know she's not trying to seduce me. She's only done that because she's blushing so hard that she needs the heavy curtain of her hair to shield her face, but tell that to my twitching cock who apparently thinks this is a striptease.

"Well, you snored just a little bit. It was fucking cute." I take the hair tie she's playing with and slip it around my wrist because I want her hands on me, and I have no doubts that she'll take the bait.

She reaches around my wrist to get her hair band back, but I lay my hand flat on hers to keep it there.

"Okay, talk to me, Tess. What's the problem with that night?"

"I couldn't...we really can't do that again."

"Why the hell not?" I ask, already gearing up to convince her otherwise.

"Nathan, KidStation is the biggest campaign I've ever managed. Heck, it's the only one I've ever led, and it's also my first opportunity to do so. I shouldn't even have been asked to do it as an undergrad."

She slips her band off my wrist and removes her hand from mine. "I would really like to use it for my finals. It's potentially a history-making campaign. The kind that could help me graduate with honors."

"Absolutely, Tess. I don't see you bagging anything less," I agree, my chest swelling with a mix of admiration and desire.

She tucks her hair behind her ear, smiling demurely at my praise. "Also, Guardian Angels Network is relying on me to pull this project off. It'll mean the world to them. So, you see why I can't let anything jeopardize this."

Like sleeping with the boss.

Fuck. I can't argue with that.

The fact that she's put her professional obligations before her own obvious needs only makes me crave her more.

Double fuck.

I have no clue how I'll keep my hands off her, but if it means that much to her, then I'll have to try.

"I completely understand, Tess, and I respect that. But if you ever call me Dr. King again, all bets are off."

She chuckles. "Why? Do you hate being called that?"

"Not at all. It's a rule just for you. Break it, and our don't-touch pact goes out the window."

Because I recently found out I have a fetish: the sound of my name on your tongue.

"Okay," she agrees, smiling.

"And, Tess?"

"Yes?"

"Don't hide what you feel from me. If you want or don't want something, talk to me about it."

She considers my request, and even though I can tell she wants to argue, she inclines her head in agreement. "Alright."

I feel the tension of the past week finally leaving me. As much as I want her naked and writhing under me, I also want her seeking me out because she wants to talk to me about anything and everything.

While being her lover would be amazing, being her confidant sounds equally appealing, just in a different way.

"So, is there anything else waiting for you in Boston? Besides top honors and job offers that'll make the Guardian Angels look like small fry?"

She grins, clearly looking forward to achieving all that. "Anything else like what?"

"Like a boyfriend."

She freezes, no doubt re-calibrating and asking herself if we are really having *that* talk.

When she takes too long to answer, I ask again, "Are you dating some guy back in Boston?"

She slowly shakes her head. "No."

I release the breath I hadn't realized I was holding. Although, it's pretty selfish of me to want her single since I have no intention of dating her myself.

She turns the question back to me. "What about you? Anyone likely to slash my Trek bike tires for being with you last week?"

I almost spit out my coffee. "Jesus, Tess! What sort of women do you think I date?"

She shrugs, smirking. "I dunno. The sort you shouldn't cross by messing around with their men?"

"Why—what would make you think that?" I'm really curious to know what gave her that idea about me.

"I just think it takes a certain kind of woman to be with you."

I'm so intrigued right now, I can't even hide it. "Go on."

She takes a sip of her coffee. "First, you're a single and very successful doctor in your forties. Meaning, you're jaded, and it takes a lot to turn your head. Therefore, I'm thinking she'd have to be more than just a pretty face or sexy body. She'd have to be really smart to grab and keep your attention."

"Okay, I'll allow that. What's your second point?"

"Well, you have a way of being very direct, which can skate pretty close to icy at times. So, she needs to be able to toss the puck right back—no shrinking violets here. I'm betting she's got a bit of fire in her, a spine of steel. Maybe even a mean streak."

She moves on to the next point when I just stare at her.

"And, finally, you're...very attractive. And good in bed. Meaning, she's probably obsessed with you."

I cock my head to look at Tess like she's an alien. "Your imagination is wild as fuck, Tess."

"You have no idea." She grins, flashing the dimples in her cheeks. "I even have a picture of what she'd look like."

My eyebrows fly to my hairline, and I fold my arms in wonder. "Pray tell!"

"Jet-black hair would be my first guess."

I shake my head in disappointment. "I'm afraid you're wrong, baby. She's blonde."

"Really?" And then, as if just realizing what I said, she shoots me a crestfallen look. "You're seeing someone?"

"Yes. She's blonde. With green eyes."

"No way."

"She actually looks a lot like you, Tess. The resemblance is uncanny."

"Stop!" Seeming to catch onto the joke, she laughs.

"It's true. You just described yourself, Tess."

"But... but... I don't have a mean streak!" she sputters.

"Maybe not, but you're certainly obsessed with me."

"I am not!"

"Aren't you?" I lift a single eyebrow, and without me saying anything, she blushes, no doubt remembering what she confessed to me while she was mindless with desire.

"I, um... refuse to be held accountable for anything I said while under your influence."

Fire leaps up in my groin, but I take pity on her and let her off the hook, for now. "Fair enough." I smile into my coffee.

Clearly, she's not done with our conversation because she dives straight back in. "So, I've often wondered why you didn't marry. Didn't you ever find someone?"

I freeze. This part of my life isn't usually up for discussion with anyone besides my mother, and my first instinct is to shut down the line of questioning. However, when I look at her, what I see in her warm gaze makes me want to give her the answers she's searching for.

So, I put my cup aside to give her my complete attention.

"Marriage isn't something I'm inclined to do. Love or relationships, either. So, no, Tess, I don't have a girlfriend. I never have, actually."

Her mouth opens in an "O" shape. "But why?"

I debate telling her the truth, but in the end, I decide that I probably should. Not just for her sake, but because I need it said out loud so I can hear myself reaffirming why this little obsession with Tess cannot be more than a passing fling.

I speak fast before I can change my mind. "Someone very close to me fell in love with a girl when we were in our teens. It was one of those epic, thunderstruck moments. But it was doomed to fail from the start."

"How so?"

"First, it took him away from me. For eighteen years, we were inseparable, and then, this girl showed up. Suddenly, I lost him before I even processed what was happening."

Her eyes widen in shock. "But... isn't that what happens when you find someone? They take priority over your friends?"

Shaking my head, I force myself to look away and temper my words. "Not if the need for that person makes you lose yourself. His need stripped him of his dignity. Broke him into pieces."

"Oh, my God, Nathan, I'm so very sorry."

"It's alright, Tess."

"Is that the reason why—?"

I know what she's about to say, so I nod. "What I experienced through him was enough to turn me off relationships for the rest of my life. I can't ever put myself in a position to get sucked into that toxicity of needing someone so badly that I can't think rationally."

"It wasn't your friend's fault," Tess murmurs. "If the girl truly loved him, she would never let him lose himself. That's what a relationship should be: looking out for your partner because you know they're too invested in you to look out for themselves."

I tilt my head to the side, looking at her as though I'm just seeing her for the first time.

"Are you sure you're just twenty-six, baby?"

She laughs. "I know. I'm great with giving relationship advice, just not the best at taking them. My friends say that all the time."

"Friends back in Boston?" I question, curious to know more about her life before she came here.

"Funny, I haven't made an awful lot of friends in Boston. They're mostly here in LA."

The corner of her mouth lifts in a sexy smirk. "I became too busy chasing success, after a certain grouch read me the riot act for giving him such a raging hard-on that he could hardly walk straight."

I throw back my head and laugh. The sound catches her by surprise, and it occurs to me she's probably never heard me laugh. I suppose I'm a bit of a grouch, then.

As my laughter settles into chuckles, I catch the sultry look on her face. Biting her lip, her gaze runs over me like a caress until her eyes finally meet mine.

She's turned on. Very turned on. *Fuck me.*

"Tess," I begin, already seeing our no-touch pact erupting into flames and thinking we're going to need another plan.

Her ringing phone interrupts me, and she stands so she can fish it out of the back pocket of her pants. I never thought I'd see the day when wrinkled hospital scrubs would send a bolt of lust through me, but here I am.

"Hi," she murmurs, sitting back down.

I watch Tessa's anxiety level mount as the call progresses, and her delicate hand resting on the table curls into a fist. I suppress the urge to cover it with mine in a silent show of support.

"Is it your father?" I mouth, but she shakes her head no. She listens to the person on the other end a bit more, and with each passing moment, she becomes more and more upset.

"I-I guess I could come down now. Alright, I'll be there soon." She slowly hangs up and keeps looking at her phone screen even after she does so.

"Something just came up. Nathan, I'm afraid I have to go." She doesn't raise her head to look at me as she says it.

I can only stare at her, surprised she'd think that I'd let her go without finding out more about what is going on and if she'd be okay dealing with it on her own.

"Are you going to tell me what that call was about?" I finally ask when she looks up.

"That was Valencia PD on the phone. Major Crimes Department. It's about my mom."

Slivers of anxiety run down my spine. "What about her?"

"It's... gosh, it's really hard to say out loud. It's what I was arguing with my dad about the other night."

Unable to resist touching her any longer, I hold out my hand for hers. "Give me your hand."

She slips her palm in mine, and I apply the smallest bit of pressure to her pulse point.

"Talk to me, Tess."

She nods. "Okay. So, last month, the police told me that they were reopening her case. They found evidence in some journals she kept to show that her death may not have been accidental."

The fuck?

I try to keep my tone of voice measured when I ask, "Are they implying that it was suicide?"

"Or murder. And the key to which one lies in those journals, apparently."

"I see. And have you read them?"

She looks almost terrified at the thought. "I've... started. It's a lot to take in. Every time I try to get into it, I get goosebumps. It's like she knew something was going to happen, and her words are so different from the ones she used while she was still alive. Like she was a completely different person to the one I knew."

"Who did you know?"

She takes a moment to consider her response, then admits, "She was kind. She never raised her voice, but she was never really excited about much as well. She wrote cookbooks and published them under a pen name."

"What name?"

"Mae White."

Figures.

"There was something... different about her. She was closed off. Don't get me wrong, she was always full of encouragement for me, always telling me to go after what I wanted, but she never gave much of herself. I never knew what exactly she was thinking, and I don't think my dad did, either. I suppose that's why he felt the need to cheat?"

"There's no excuse for crossing that line, Tess."

She sighs in agreement. "I know. I just...I felt like such a failure, so sometimes, it's easier to blame her. Like she stubbornly kept her innermost thoughts and personality away from me. It's easier to be upset with her than with myself for not being able to help her."

Dismay at her admission overcomes me, and I squeeze her hand tighter at the thought that she blames herself.

"Excuse me? You were eleven. Why on earth would you feel responsible for someone else's emotions?"

In all the years I've known her and all the times she had confided in me about her home life, Tess has never once told me how she truly felt about her mother until now.

Tess takes a deep breath before continuing her explanation, "When John picked me from the orphanage, he said Mom had wanted a much younger child, but they picked me because they were told that I was great at making people feel good. He wanted me to make my mother happy."

My free hand curls into a fist, my knuckles whitening in rage. "He told you that?"

She nods.

"He's a sick, demented asshole. What kind of a person would force that level of responsibility onto a child?"

John made Tess think that she owed him for adopting her, and it sounds like he made sure that she never forgot why he had made her his daughter in the first place.

She doesn't argue with my assessment of her father, only shrugs and continues, "I was just happy to finally have parents and be a normal kid. Anyway, at first, my dad and I were really close, and he was the perfect dad. And since Mom hardly left the house, my dad took me everywhere—school, camps, recitals…

She looks at me. "But with every passing year, when Mom stayed the same, his attitude became colder. Nathan, he kept reminding me that I was adopted for a reason."

Sensing that there's more to her story, I observe the way she fidgets in her chair and tucks her hair behind her ear with her free hand.

"He's a fucking prick, Tess, and a horrible excuse for a parent."

"I, um…sort of realize that now," she states solemnly.

I say softly, "That being said, though, do you think he's capable of murder? Or your mom of suicide?"

"I always thought she was depressed. But having done a minor in psychology, I'm not so sure. Nathan, it almost felt like she was blocking something out. Like she was choosing to live on the sidelines…perhaps because she'd suffered some trauma from living life fully. But there was a certain defiance in her. I never would have guessed that she'd actually do it, but I could be wrong."

I only watch Tess, astounded by how intuitive and perceptive she is, captivated by how her mind works.

I could sit and listen to her talk all day. I ignore the alarm bells ringing in my head about how much I like every little thing I'm discovering about her and continue asking about her parents.

"And your father? Would you say he's remotely capable of something like that?"

"I don't see why he would need to hurt her. Mom never antagonized him. I don't ever recall them arguing...well, except for that one time." Her cheeks turn pink at the memory.

"What happened?"

"It was when you—um, the Fount—took interest in our high school charity club and invited us to see you."

"Okay?" My sentence drifts off, an unsaid "and?" floating between us.

"Well, I told Mom about it, and it's one of the times I remember her actually getting excited about anything. She was proud of me and told me to go. So, when I got back home and started blabbing about how incredible it was meeting you, my dad overheard, and he flew off the handle. I'd never seen him so angry."

She trails off, but after I give her hand another encouraging squeeze, she continues, "But Mom laughed in his face, told me to make sure I always go after what I wanted, and walked out of the room, leaving my dad sputtering after her."

She smiles as if she finds the memories amusing.

"My dad tried banning me from the club, but it was hard since I was the club president. To answer your question, my dad can get irrationally angry, but I don't think he's capable of murder. I suppose I'll have to wait and see what the detectives think since they said they found something else in the journals today."

More tension seeps into my shoulders. "What did they find?" I ask, a little too quickly.

Tessa doesn't seem to notice. "Dunno. That's why I need to go find out."

I take a deep breath. I don't usually make split-second decisions, but I've been waiting for this news for a long time. Way longer than even Tessa can imagine.

"I'm coming with you," I tell her.

Chapter Ten

TESSA

"Thank you for coming in so quickly, Ms. Blackwell, and Dr. King, it's good to have you here, too." Detective Warner offers us seats at the crowded desk at the Major Crimes Unit office.

He then introduces his partner, who I've never met before, a wiry brunette with the name "Vause" stitched on her uniform. "This is Detective Angela Vause. She specializes in behavioral analysis and will be assisting us with this case."

I hide my trembling fingers in a fist as I offer a tremulous smile in return.

"Detective Vause has been going through your mom's journals and was hoping you might be able to help us fill in some blanks."

I immediately shake my head. "Um, I'm not sure how much help I'll be there. I've only started reading them." *And they're leaving me with more questions than answers as it is.*

Initially, I wasn't going to get into those journals until after I'd returned to Boston, but with the Fount job, I couldn't very well delay things for three months. Still, I stalled until last week after seeing my dad again.

His cruel dismissal of what could be Mom's tortured, fevered final moments and how defensive he got when I brought up the journals made me wonder if he was desperate to shut this whole idea down.

His behavior also made me question if he would have destroyed the journals had he known about them. It piqued my interest in the entries, and I found myself reading them whenever I had a free moment.

But it's been hard reading them alone, not to mention scary. I was tempted to call Nathan a few times, but I didn't want him to think of me as too needy.

Now, after having him drop everything to come here to sit next to me and have his big hand hold mine, one of his fingers gently stroking the rapid pulse in my wrist, I realize that I was wrong about him.

Nathan would have wanted me to call him, and he wouldn't have hesitated to give me any support I needed.

Vause reaches into the desk and pulls up some leather and hardbound books that look like they've been around for decades, then a sheet of paper with clean handwriting on it.

"These are the original journals that Detective Warner made copies of and gave to yourself and Mr. Blackwell. Now, I've gone through the journals and narrowed down the ones that are most relevant to this case."

I nod, and she continues, "They span over a twenty-year period, but her entries start to take a darker turn in the final six years of her life."

She picks up a shiny, black leather-bound book, which looks to be in a better state than the others. "And in the six months before her death, it's almost impossible to make sense of her words."

I feel Nathan's hand move to my thigh, a solid warmth that grounds me. I don't realize that I'm nervously tapping my foot until he gives my leg a gentle pat. I force myself to remain still in my seat, putting my hand on top of his.

I need to deal with wherever this investigation leads. It's the only way to move on.

I told him everything I know about the case on the hour-long drive here and some more things about my parents, noticing that the more I revealed, the calmer he got. Afterwards, he just took hold of my hand and hasn't let mine go up until now, but he still makes sure to offer me a supportive touch.

"How many journals do you have altogether, Detective?" Nathan's deep voice interrupts my anxiety. He gives me a quick reassuring smile when I turn to him, then focuses back on the two detectives sitting across the cluttered desk.

I'd been reluctant to have him accompany me, but I'm now glad that I let him because he seems genuinely interested, and unlike me, he has the presence of mind to ask important questions.

"More than a dozen," Warner replies. "It's just that a lot of it is either indecipherable or sound like the ramblings of a deranged woman—"

A shrill ringing interrupts Warner, making me flinch. It's coming from his belt. He quickly kills the ringing, then excuses himself, stepping outside the room to answer the call.

"Forgive my colleague's language," a red-faced Vause apologizes. "We are hard-pressed to get it right this time, so it is frustrating that the information isn't as straightforward as we'd all like it to be."

I just wish they'd get on with it, so I can leave and put the past behind me once and for all.

Her eyes soften as she looks at me. "This is a sleepy town. The thought that this case could be anything but an accident will attract a lot of unwanted attention, which can damage the case, so we need to tread carefully."

"Right. So, what do you have so far?" Nathan nudges the woman to get to the point, and I give his hand a grateful squeeze.

Vause pulls a pen from her breast pocket and holds it steady over a notepad.

"Mary never gave any names, but it seemed like right from the beginning and up to the time of her death, there were one or two other men in her life aside from John, and she seemed afraid of at least one of them. If she was murdered, any of them might have been responsible."

"Okay." I digest that information. My dad had never tried to hide his mistresses from me, but hearing that Mom may have had affairs as well shocks me.

She always seemed so involved in her hobbies and locked away in her own mind to be running around with another man. She hardly even left the house.

"The first entry she wrote was when she was in high school. And the last was on the day she died. Both are eerily similar, even though they're twenty years apart."

"Similar how?" I ask.

"In the style of writing and what she chose to put in upper case. In both, she seemed happy, excited even. The first was to marry someone, and the second was to meet someone."

Nathan hears my soft gasp of pain and gently squeezes my hand. "I'm here, baby. Breathe."

Vause looks at us both, but nothing in her expression changes. I know she has made a quick assessment of the relationship between Nathan and me. I'm not sure if that's a good or bad thing, or if her assumptions will come back to haunt me later. I force the thought out of my head, telling myself to deal with the here and now.

"Those are the facts we're working with so far." She takes a fresh sheet of paper and scribbles on it. "Ms. Blackwell, what can you tell me about your parents' relationship?"

"What do you want to know about it?"

"Did they fight or argue a lot? Did your dad ever threaten her?"

"Um, no," I say. "They *barely* spoke. Each was content to do their own thing. Mom was often engrossed in her cookbooks, and my dad, well, when he wasn't out with other people, he'd be in the lab. I guess I did the talking and arguing for everyone."

"Hmm." Vause flips through a few pages of my mom's diary. "Lab, you said? I thought he was a farmer?"

"Yes. But there's a place we—the Blackwells—call the 'lab' in the Circle Orchard, the oldest and largest property our family owns."

One of the two still owned by my dad. The rest have been sold off over the years. To Nathan, it would seem.

My dad didn't seem to care about losing the other farms as long as the Circle Orchard remained, but recalling the animosity between the two of them at the engagement party, he probably cared more than he let on, but he just needed the money more.

I hesitate revealing a family trade secret, but I decide there's no sense in hiding anything at this point. The police would eventually find out, anyway.

"Apparently, there is a secret ingredient that one of the Blackwells accidentally discovered decades ago that almost infinitely preserves perishables."

Vause is scribbling like mad. "Okay. Tell me more about this ingredient."

"Um…it's top secret, and it's called CX3, I think. We—I mean, my dad and his dad before him—believe it could be worth more than gold if successfully refined. Personally, I think it's a hoax, but they believe it works, but it's just very 'unstable.'"

"Unstable in what way?" Nathan has gone still, and even his finger has stopped stroking my skin, but when I glance at him, he gives me a reassuring smile. It doesn't reach his eyes.

He finds this news upsetting.

"I have no clue," I tell him truthfully, watching as his eyes burn with something dark. "I assumed that it's maybe toxic in some way. I don't know if it's now been approved, but my dad was obsessed about getting it to a marketable quality at some point."

Nathan's rigid posture tells me he knows something that he's not saying.

He knows my parents for sure, and not just as acquaintances from the same small hometown. They attended high school together, and they seem to have a deeper history of bad blood between them.

Before I can question him about it further, Vause continues, "Thank you, Ms. Blackwell. We will certainly follow that lead. Now, I know that you were away in college during the last year of your mom's life, but do you have any idea if she was seeing someone else?"

"You think she had an affair?" *That her lover killed her?*

"It looks like she did."

"Why would you think she had an affair?" Nathan's almost lazy drawl belies the tension I can feel vibrating from him.

Vause looks up at him. "Because, Dr. King, in an uncharacteristic moment of lucidity, she mentions something recognizable. Apart from Tessa's name, which had come up a few times in several entries, she mentions Lake Orange in a way that makes it sound like she might have been meeting with someone at the lake."

Nathan drops my hand, choosing to clasp both of his in his lap. This time, when I look up at him, he doesn't look back.

Suddenly feeling alone, I focus back on the task at hand. "What does that mean?"

"It means that we might have been right to reopen the case. Yes, Mary Blackwell was depressed, possibly schizophrenic, but her journals are not a mad woman's rambling like her husband claims."

The detective's angular face swims before me as hot tears spring to my eyes. I have to agree.

Mary Blackwell wasn't mad. She was deeply traumatized, and no one could help her. Or rather, she wouldn't let anyone help her.

"There are enough clues in the writings, but only if you are close enough to her to figure out what she truly meant, which is where you come in, Ms. Blackwell." Vause notices the tears I'm subtly dabbing at and says in a concerned tone, "Ms. Blackwell? Tessa?"

"I'm good, I'm alright," I say while choking back a sob.

Vause goes to the sink on the far side of the room, presumably to get some tissues for me, but Nathan hands me a white handkerchief.

I don't want a hanky right now. I want you to hold me and tell me that I'm not alone in this nightmare.

I take it, though, and press it to my nose, inhaling Nathan's earthy and spicy smell. "Thanks."

Vause returns with the tissues and places them on the desk. "So, you haven't quite made it halfway through the entries yet?"

I shake my head.

"I think you should try. I'm certain that you'll find a lot of clues in there. But just to help you find some motivation to get through it, I'll tell you something else we've found out just by combing through those entries."

I nod and gesture for her to continue. "Okay."

"First, we know that she attended high school with John and that they fell in love in their senior year—"

"Wrong."

We both whip our heads in unison to face Nathan, who is sitting so stiffly, he might have been chiseled out of granite.

"Dr. King?" Vause questions.

Nathan cuts his gaze to her. "They didn't *fall in love* in senior year of high school. They didn't fall in love at all."

Vause narrows her eyes at him. "We have school records and eyewitness accounts that Mary Archer met John Blackwell in high school," she challenges.

Nathan's eyes darken. "Of course they met in high school. I went to high school with them, too, so it figures that we all met there, doesn't it? I'm saying it wasn't John Blackwell who Mary was in love with."

I only stare at Nathan with a chill running down my spine, waiting with bated breath for him to say more. Dreading what he would say next.

Was Mom in love with... *Nathan?*

Nathan isn't even looking at me. His eyes are locked on Vause, whose nostrils are flared. Still staring at Nathan, she plunges her hand into the pile of journals, picking one up randomly and flipping through the pages.

"Here," Vause insists, "this is Mary's entry from August 20, 1996, the first day of senior year."

My immediate thought is to sprint out of the room, cover my ears, or let out a loud wail. Anything to stop myself from hearing my mom's thoughts before I can even prepare myself for them. But before I can think of what to do, Vause is already reading.

"'I was sure that I was going to hate this school, too. Pretty, pretty sure. But it turned out that Fate had other plans. Because today, I met him. There was a spider in my locker, and I ran right into this solid, warm, citrus-smelling tower of muscle. I saw him and everything in my world stopped. Black simply looked at me for a full minute, then just walked away with a knowing smile. And I know, too. What we're going to do.'"

Vause pauses. "And this last part is in all caps," she informs us before continuing to read." "'GET MARRIED. RIGHT AFTER HIGH SCHOOL. OR DIE TRYING.'"

I stare, barely seeing anything. Although my heart is breaking, I have to agree with Nathan. It's hard to imagine Mom was ever this deeply in love with my dad, not after all the years I witnessed them being so cold and callous to one another.

"See?" Vause says, slamming the book shut. "She never mentions him by name, only calls him 'Black.' But she *does* marry John Blackwell immediately after graduation."

That assumption makes sense. I glance at Nathan, already done with this insane argument and just want to move on. But his jaw is still tight, and his eyes are pools of molten blue fire.

"Mary wasn't talking about John."

Vause lets out a rattled sigh. "Dr. King, as much as I—"

"Black wasn't John Blackwell," he snaps.

I can't believe the way Nathan is reacting right now. He has a white-knuckled grip on the chair's arm, and there's a slight sheen of sweat on his forehead.

He appears… flustered. More than even I was a few minutes ago.

The only other time I've seen him lose his cool was on the night of the engagement party. When my dad was trashing Mom.

"Who was Black, then, Nathan?" I ask, dreading the answer.

He takes his sweet time answering, most likely debating whether to say anything at all.

"Black was my twin brother, Ciaran King."

Chapter Eleven

NATHAN

CHAPTER ELEVEN – NATHAN

The ride back to LA is silent, with Tess mostly staring out through the window or scrolling through her phone, her body language closed off and anger rolling off her in waves.

More times than I can count, I almost pull over so I could get her to speak to me, but if I'm being honest, my thoughts are also all over the place.

The last thing I expected when I sought Tess out earlier today was to be sucked right into the deadly love triangle that put me off of relationships for life.

So, what the hell am I doing craving a woman who reminds me of everything I loathe? Wanting her eyes on me and yearning to see her smile are probably the most idiotic things I could crave right now, but knowing how stupid it is doesn't stop my need for her.

I watch her profile now to see that she's typing something on her phone.

"Baby?"

She looks up at me but doesn't respond.

"Are you okay?"

"Sure. Amazing. Why wouldn't I be?" With that reply, she goes back to typing.

Fuck. She's livid, and she has every right to be. I'm sure I would be reacting much worse if I were in her position.

"I don't know, you tell me. You're silent and tense as a drawn bowstring."

"I'm just busy catching up with work." Lifting her phone in the air slightly, she still keeps the majority of her attention on the screen.

"Alright." I leave her to it, and at some point, I think I hear her grind her teeth.

When we reach her apartment complex, I deliberately drive into the basement parking lot, so we can have some privacy. I get out of the car and round the hood toward her side, but she's already getting out.

As she tries to walk past me, I gently splay my hand on her belly to stop her.

"Tess, you're angry, and I get why. Will you at least talk to me?"

"Thanks for the ride, Nathan, and offering support when I needed it. But I'm tired." She reaches up on her tiptoes, gives me a small peck on my jaw that I feel all the way to my feet, then slips away before I can stop her again.

Chapter Twelve

NATHAN

One Week Later

I step into the largest function room on the top floor of the Fount, and in spite of my foul mood, I find my face splitting into a reluctant smile when I see the decor and the makeshift stage set up.

The remissions unit, given half a chance, would throw a party every other weekend, their excuse being that it's for the patients, but really, it's because Jackson Ames is a real party animal. Jackson has outdone himself this time, bringing in the famous Ninth Life band.

The reasons why the board allows these "rem" parties keeps piling up every year. They're brief, don't interfere with work hours, are alcohol-free, and are an absolute hit with patients.

Most importantly, they're self-sustaining. Not to mention, hospitals all over California are starting to emulate us.

Jackson and his unit somehow find a way to raise money for these gigs, without fail, every single time.

I came here because I knew Tess would be here. It's been a week since I dropped her off at her apartment. I haven't spoken to her in all that time, and I'm going crazy.

I take a cursory look around, trying to stem the disappointment when I don't see her anywhere.

"Dr. King! So glad you could make it!" Jackson hands me an iced tea with a lemon slice impaled on the rim of the glass. He's flanked by Gary Moore, one of the palliative specialist nurses.

"*People* are starting to think that we do these parties for the sake of them." Jackson's emphasis isn't lost on us.

Gary hides his snort in his drink, but Jackson only glares at him before continuing his speech. "So, when someone like the Chief MD shows up, it gives us the validation we need so those *people* don't keep looking down their noses at us."

Jackson and Gary are married, but I don't attempt to understand how they navigate their relationship since they always seem to argue nonstop.

"I didn't realize you guys needed validation," Gary scoffs.

"Well, of course not, but some *people* really need to get off their high horses and quit making us feel bad for surviving."

Gary shoots him a narrow-eyed glare, but judging by the playful glint in his eyes, there's no malice behind his expression. "We're fucking dying, asshole. Y'all need to be kicked up your fucking smug asses."

"Yet, here you are with the hedonists," Jackson points out.

"I'm only here for the music, Jack," Gary grumbles. "It is Ninth Life, after all."

"Yeah, makes sense. It must be so convenient to be able to lay down and pick up that cloak of judgment at will. In fact, I think I need one for myself, too."

Gary takes a step closer to his partner and murmurs, "Prick. What you need is a good—"

"Guys," I interrupt before it turns into one of those arguments they often have to take to another room to "finish."

"Anyway, Jackson," I ask, "which bank did you rob to get Ninth Life to come?"

"Well, believe it or not, the Charlies, ahem, I mean, the Guardian Angels, arranged for them to play tonight. I mean, talk about a solid charity."

My jaw drops open in surprise. "Seriously?"

"I know, right? Personally, I don't think there's anything she can't do." He gestures toward the back of the room, and I whip my head around to see none other than Tess as she steps into the large hall, her arms full of what looks like disposable plates.

My eyes eagerly follow her to the buffet stand, where she drops the plates, then she makes her way toward the front to join her team in applauding as Ninth Life finishes a song.

I feel two pairs of eyes on me, so I quickly tear my gaze away from Tess and casually scan the crowd before returning my attention back to the band on the stage.

"You know, someone needs to do something about getting that woman to stay here permanently." Jackson nudges me, wagging his eyebrows meaningfully.

Then, as if to remove all doubt as to who he means, he jerks his head toward the far side of the room where Tessa and the Guardian Angels team are now chatting away with staff and patients.

As though she feels my gaze on her, she looks over here. I feel a jolt of triumph when her gaze snags on me, and she does a double take, effectively losing track of what she was saying.

Then, she seems to shake herself out of a daze before continuing speaking.

Jackson clucks his tongue and gives me that annoying nudge again. "Surely, I can't be expected to do everything around here. Besides, I'm already spoken for. This one is on you, Dr. King."

My smile drops when I get his meaning. "Jackson Ames…"

"Just my two cents, boss. Anyway, enjoy the party and the music, which is likely to burst our eardrums by the end of the night, but will be totally worth the ENT consults from Pacific Coast."

With those parting words, he walks off with Gary watching him go, and I heave a deep breath as I turn back to the sight in front of me. There's no longer any point in hiding the fact that I only have eyes for Tess tonight.

"I'm afraid this time, I have to agree with him, Doctor. She's not the type of woman you let go of, if you know what I mean," Gary's solemn announcement adds a tone of finality to the conversation, cementing what his partner playfully suggested.

Why, all of a sudden, everyone feels the need to give me relationship advice is beyond me.

I suppose it's futile to try hiding anything from these guys since they've been working with me for the past decade, and I've discovered that nothing ever gets past these two.

It's an after-work party, and apart from the guests of honor—the patients themselves— the staff are dressed in work clothes, and a few are in scrubs straight from the OR, presumably wanting to grab a bite to eat and see the Ninth Life perform before heading home.

Tess is wearing a simple black Guardian Angels T-shirt and jeans, but it's suddenly the most provocative attire I've ever seen.

And apparently, I'm not the only one who thinks so because one of the Ninth Life band members, a devilishly handsome guy, leaves the stage in between sets to start to chat her up.

He's standing a tad too close and sporting an idiotic smile. The worst part is that she's smiling back at him.

My legs are already moving me toward them before I even fully process what I'm doing, or the fact that Tess is still boiling mad at me and didn't say more than ten words to me on the drive back from Valencia.

Nor since then, and it's been a week.

I could have squashed this whole drama. I could have gone to her, groveled, and told her everything I know about Mary, but I wasn't quite prepared to let go of the guilt, the pain, and, yes, the blazing rage.

To be fair, I also didn't think it would be important to my psychological well-being to remain on speaking terms with a woman I'm not sleeping with.

The last time I went out of town for a week, I missed her terribly, and I reasoned that it was due to the physical distance.

Now, it's the mere thought of her being angry with me that is driving me up the wall.

I watch as she returns the goof's smile, seeming to encourage his obvious flirting.

She controls her reaction better this time when she sees me approaching, which annoys me to no end.

I want her to be soft, open, and completely defenseless because that's how she's making me feel right now.

"—should catch up while you're here, Tessa." I catch the tail end of what the band guy just told her.

"That would be amazing," she agrees when I finally reach them.

"Hello, Tess." Perhaps it's the fact that we've got company or because I haven't been this close to her in a week, but I slip my arm around her waist and gently pull her into me as if it's the most natural thing to do.

"Hey, Nathan." Is it just my wishful thinking, or does she lean into me? We both look at the guy who is now observing us with interest.

"Chris, this is Nathan King, he's the Chief MD and a friend. Nathan, Christopher Dean, lead guitarist for Ninth Life. Chris's sister and I went to UCLA together," Tess explains, waving her hand between us while making the introductions.

I release the breath that I didn't realize I was holding until now.

He's Tess's friend's brother. That should make her off-limits, right? He shouldn't be interested in her.

Just like the man who's almost twice her age and is the twin brother of her mother's ex-lover shouldn't be interested in her? My mind taunts.

"Very nice to meet you, Nathan." With his polite but even expression, I can't tell if he's genuine or not.

I decide to play nice as well. "Much obliged. Thank you for coming here. Our patients will not forget this party for a long while, that's for sure."

"Oh, Tessa knows I have no willpower to refuse her anything she wants." He winks at Tess.

My smile dies.

Or maybe not so off-limits, after all.

An awkward beat of silence hangs in the air between us as the atmosphere separating Chris and me goes arctic.

Then, with a smirk that I'd like to wipe off his face with my fist, Chris says to Tess in a low voice, "Told ya. See you later, Nathan!" He then disappears to mingle with the other guests.

I turn around to face Tess, a shocked expression on my face. "What the hell was that?" I demand.

She scoffs like she can't believe what nerve I have to be asking anything of her. "What do you want, Nathan?" Pulling the rest of the way out of my hold, she looks me up and down in a calculating manner, like she's trying to figure me out.

"Tess, come on. What do you mean, what do I want?"

She lifts her brows, then her mouth hardens. "I don't have the foggiest clue what you want from me, Nathan."

"Let's not do this here." I put my hand on the small of her back and start to lead her out of the room, but she stops me.

"Exactly, not here. So, take your hands off me. I told you I don't want us to look like we're a thing."

"You're still angry, I know. We should go talk and hash everything out."

She rears back in surprise. "Oh, now you want to talk. You had one whole hour on the drive back to LA to explain, and you refused to say anything to me then, but all of a sudden, now is the ideal time?"

She has me there. I try to come up with a good response, but all I manage to get out is, "I was... reeling back then. On the drive from the police station."

"And you think that I wasn't? Tell me something, did you come over here because you really wanted to talk, or because you saw me with Chris?" She crosses her arm across her chest and spreads her legs slightly apart, looking like she's preparing for a fight.

All my life, I've never had a woman dissect my actions before or ask me questions that are suddenly harder to answer than human biochemistry. It aggravates, yet arouses me to no end.

"Does it matter?"

She raises a single eyebrow in response. Knowing just how stubborn she can be, I release a deep breath and prepare to tell her the truth.

"Fine, it was both. But you know the reason I came here at all is because of you. I missed you." It feels good to admit it, as if a weight has been lifted off my shoulders.

She looks at me like I've grown two heads. "It took you one week to realize that?"

Fuck. She's making me work for this apology. "Tessa, don't make it harder than it needs to be. I'm trying to sort things out between us. I was reeling, you were angry, and I thought you needed some space. But giving you time obviously isn't helping."

Rolling her eyes, she gives me a bland look. "Oh, really? Did it occur to you to ask me what I thought or what I wanted instead of making the decision for me?"

I take a calming breath. I'm about this close to dragging her into an empty room and fucking her until she screams, her wishes to remain unattached be damned. "Alright, Tess. What do you want?"

She looks at me like a teacher would a particularly dull student.

Scratch that. Spank her until she begs me to fuck her, then fuck her until she screams.

"What do I want? Nothing. You can do whatever you want, as long as you don't expect me to be open and honest with you while you keep yourself tucked far away because you're afraid to get hurt."

Her words are like shards of light, hitting me in those cold, dark recesses I try not to think about, let alone acknowledge. Places I never let anyone into. My usual response in a situation like this one is to completely shut down and walk away.

To disconnect before I end up in a toxic spiral. Like Ciaran did.

But this is Tessa. I don't think I could get away from her, even if I wanted to. She's like a stubborn weed growing inside my otherwise cold, barren heart.

"This ends now," I growl, ignoring the warning bells in my head. "We're going somewhere to talk, right now."

"Like hell we are. I'm having fun," she snaps.

"Listen, Tess, you can either come with me, or we can make a scene. Your choice."

She looks around and sees that we're already drawing attention, given that I'm standing almost on top of her and our faces are shoved close to each other's.

I see the moment she realizes that she really has no choice, and I take her elbow and quickly steer her from the crowded room.

I can feel the anger radiating off her in waves.

Chapter Thirteen

NATHAN

We step into the cool, quiet hallway, and I lead her down the carpeted corridor to the paneled glass door at the end. I scan my card to open the door to the hardly-used conference room, push the door open, and gesture for her to go in.

She huffs but enters.

The moment I cross the threshold, I drag her back into me, then push her against the door and crash my lips down to hers, swallowing her surprised gasp.

The kiss is savage, full of frustration and pent-up desire. She slaps her palms against my chest, intending to push me away, but within a few moments, she changes her mind, bunching my T-shirt in her hands and pulling me closer to her instead.

Her lips open under mine, and I sweep my tongue into her mouth. Her taste and scent intoxicate me until suddenly, it's not enough.

My hand strokes down her back and around the ample curve of her butt. I pull her closer to me as I grind my aching cock against her.

I hear her throaty moans, and my control starts to splinter.

We should stop before I take her against this door. In full-view of anyone who decides to step out of the hall because the door and walls to this room are transparent.

I tear my mouth away and lean my temple against her forehead, shutting my aching balls down.

"Tess. Baby." I pant, gulping in air like I've just run a marathon.

She tries to catch her breath, clearly still affected by our kiss ."So, how did you work this out in your head? That you're just going to kiss me and I'll fall back into your arms?"

"Tess—"

"All this time, you knew. In the cafeteria, the selfish woman you were on about was my mother. Do you have any idea how stupid I felt back in that detective's office?"

I keep my tone even when I reply, "Baby, lots of people in Valencia know about your parents. People who went to high school with them all know the truth. You can't be mad at one person for not telling you a random fact about them. A fact that even the detectives could have filled you in on if they weren't born yesterday."

"But *you* were supposed to be different!" She pushes me away, practically yelling now.

I raise my brows. "How?"

"Because you're... *you*." Her fists relax, her upper lip wobbling slightly. "You *knew*. Back at the Citrus Fest five years ago, when I came on to you like an idiot."

Her voice breaks on the last word, and she turns away from me, putting her fist up against her mouth to keep a sob in. I catch the glint of a tear as it rolls down her cheek.

The image sears a hole into my heart.

"Baby." I go to her and slip my arms around her. "You're not an idiot, and you did nothing wrong. You knew what you wanted and were brave enough to go for it."

She shrugs my arms off and turns to look at me, but I continue speaking. "I'm sorry I didn't tell you about your mom. It's just that I find it extremely difficult to talk about what happened."

She nods in acknowledgment but folds her arms around her midriff, hugging herself. I see her mentally gearing herself up for what she plans to say next, and I know she still has something to get off her chest.

"Make me understand, Nathan. Did you see me as some kind of challenge?"

"A challenge?" I question, not liking the direction this conversation is going one single bit.

"My family took your land, then my dad took my mother, the one who got away from your twin brother, and so you thought you'd bang the daughter to get even?"

If she'd struck me, I wouldn't have been more shocked.

"Tess, so help me if you don't kill that theory right now, I'll spank you so hard that you won't be sitting right for weeks."

My sensual promise—or threat, depending on how she views it—doesn't faze her at all. "But something got into you that night in the limo. You and my dad argued about my mom, and all of a sudden, you were all over me. Something got you riled up. I thought it was me you wanted. Apparently, I was wrong."

I huff out a disbelieving breath. "Tess, do not talk to me about wanting. Want is too tame a word for what I feel. Do you have any idea how hard it's been staying away from you since that night?"

I grab her hand and hold it against my crotch. "I'm hard as a rock all the time, jacking off to thoughts of you multiple times a day like a goddamned teenager. I'm literally shaking with the need to sink myself balls deep inside you."

I should have been repulsed at the physical representation of the woman whose love damned Ciaran. I should not be getting all over the same woman's daughter, aching for her like an addict craving his next hit.

"I needed comfort and an outlet for my rage, Tess, just like you did for your hurt."

Her breath hitches at my fevered words, but her reply slices into me. "How do I even know that it was really your twin brother who was in love with my mom and not you?"

I level her with a look. "Because I'm alive and he's dead."

"What do you mean? I want to know everything," she demands.

I know what I should do. But it's a story I haven't told anyone, *ever*. It haunts me daily, but I've never let myself express it.

Every part of me is resisting telling her the truth. So, I keep my focus on that one tear track, on how much better Tess will feel when I tell her what I've been hiding.

I sigh as the painful memories wash over me. "Mary was a new transfer. Black, I mean Ciaran, saw her on the first day of school and fell in love instantly. I'd never seen my brother like that before."

I feel another hole sear itself in my heart as I recall my brother. *Really* recall him, the way I've not let myself do in years. I'm surprised that it doesn't hurt as much as I expect it to, especially with Tess right in front of me.

"They wanted to get married right after high school. There were financial struggles. Mary's family was very poor, and her father was in a series of huge debts."

Suddenly weary, I pull up one of the chairs by the large desk and drop into it. "We were also dirt poor, but Ciaran and I did a lot of work on the side. Mainly on the Blackwell Orchards. We did a bit of everything– cleaning, garbage collection, DIY...you name it."

"What about your father?" she asks.

"Dad died early on. Bone cancer."

After taking another deep breath, I continue to spill the truth, "Ciaran and Mary were in love, and naive enough to believe that love solved everything. Even the prospect of living in penury for the first few years while Ciaran went to med school could not change their minds."

A soft look enters her eyes. "He was going to be a doctor, too?"

I nod, then elaborate, "He was a third-year cardiology resident when he died."

"Oh, my God. What happened?" Tessa asks, her tone low.

"Just after high school, Ciaran and Mary were all over each other. They couldn't stand to be apart for more than a few hours at a time. I warned them they were moving too fast, but they just couldn't help themselves. She was often unable to wait until evening and would come visit Ciaran while we worked on the Blackwell Orchard."

"Was that when my dad saw Mom?"

I shake my head no. "He'd seen her all year but never paid any attention to her. John had his bevy of girls, and Mary wasn't his regular type. But he must have seen both of them together at some point. Seen their passion and desire. How Mary just couldn't stay away from Ciaran. And he decided he wanted her for himself."

When I take too long of a pause, Tessa comes to me, sits at the edge of the desk, and waves for me to carry on. "So, what happened after that?"

"Suddenly, Mary became preoccupied with money. How much money Ciaran was going to be making as a doctor, and how long it would take to start making it. I thought those were red flags, but there was no stopping him. Finally, Ciaran proposed to her. Mary said no."

"No!" she protests, an anguished look appearing on her face. Even though she already knows who Mary ended up marrying, she asks, "But why?"

"Turned out she was *already* engaged. To John Blackwell, the son of the wealthiest man in town."

The man whose father we worked for to save money for med school.

I want to pause, but finally getting to tell this story feels liberating; like a closed wound finally being exposed to air.

"Ciaran was broken. They'd spent the entire week before he proposed together in Ciaran's studio apartment, and she'd been engaged to another man all that time."

Tess takes a sharp breath.

"I couldn't forgive Mary for that. Ciaran was adamant that there had to be a reason why she did that and was intent on finding answers, but Mary refused to see him—either of us, actually. Because at some point I had to let go of my rage and try to help my brother win her back."

"Oh, my God Nathan, I am so sorry," Tess whispers.

I nod to acknowledge her empathy. "She and John were married the following month. Of course, we attended the wedding. Well, more like I couldn't stop Ciaran from going, so I followed to ensure that he wouldn't do anything stupid. But it was no use. She hardly spared him a glance."

"Oh, my." I see the glint of fresh tears in Tess's eyes before she quickly wipes them away with the heel of her palm.

"I've never known pain like that in my life, and it wasn't even mine to bear, it was my twin brother's. I was devastated for Ciaran and found it hard to believe that Mary chose money over love."

"But, Nathan, can't you see? There must have been a reason. You said her family was drowning in debt. Maybe Mom was under a lot of pressure to help her family out?" I see how she's struggling to accept what her mother did, and a part of me feels bad for tarnishing the memory of the one loving, albeit distant, parent she had.

"I'm afraid I can't excuse her sleeping with my brother, a man who loved her more than life itself, while being engaged to another man," I return harshly.

Tess nods slowly. I can practically see the wheels turning in her head as she digests this new piece of information about her mother, no doubt trying, and failing, to reconcile the woman she knew with the one I'm describing to her.

I continue in a rush, unable to stop the torrent of words despite knowing that she probably needs a break to deal with what she has learned.

"I kept believing that Ciaran would get over her. He had a lot going for him, you see: he was smart, ambitious, handsome. I was wrong. He spiraled out of control instead. Dropped out of med school in our third year. He eventually made it through with honors, after a couple of gap years, so I thought that he'd finally gotten over her."

Feeling restless, I stand and pace the room. This part is the most difficult for me to accept. The main reason I swore to myself never to lose myself in the pursuit of love or marriage. I shove my fisted hand into my pockets and make myself go on.

"I should have known something was very wrong when Ciaran started stalking Mary. A few years into her unhappy marriage, they had an affair, and he managed to convince Mary to leave John. She promised to. Only, she changed her mind at the last minute and instead filed a restraining order against Ciaran."

"Ciaran couldn't believe that she'd done that to him again, but he forgave her. Believe it or not, Mary and Ciaran somehow got together and started up another affair. This time, he ended up being thrown in jail for violating his restraining order."

I turn back to Tess. She just looks dazed. I start to wonder if she's been listening at all when she urges me to continue in a hollow voice, "So, was that the end for them?"

If only that were the case, he might still be alive today.

I shake my head sadly. "In time, after he got out of prison. And of course, before long they wound up seeing each other again, with the promise that Mary would leave John this time. By then, the toxicity of that relationship disgusted me, and as much as I loved my brother, I didn't want to know the details."

I come back to lean on the edge of the desk and sit close enough to Tess so our arms are touching. That small contact with her warms me, and I hope it does the same for her, too.

"Tess, my brother's life slowly bled away while he waited for his life with Mary to start. And I had to watch that.

"Of course, she broke his heart again. This time, Ciaran went to Lake Orange and never returned."

Gasping, Tess puts her hands over her face and weeps. Her pain is palpable in her stooped posture and soft, anguished sobs.

I put my arm around her shaking shoulders as my heart breaks for her. I can understand her shock and grief. I've lived with this nightmare for decades, so I'm somewhat numb to it. She is going through the emotions for the first time.

We're both silent for a few minutes, mulling over the unfortunate tragedy.

Finally, Tess murmurs, "I can't believe... I mean, Mom isn't... couldn't have done that to..."

I raise my brows, waiting for her to get her thoughts in order.

Finally, she takes a deep breath and stares at me. I'm surprised to see her eyes filled with accusation as well as tears.

"So, it was all because of them. My parents both destroyed your brother's life. How you must hate them. My mother, especially. Perhaps a part of you even resents me," she whispers.

"Come on, Tess. I don't resent you. I loved my twin brother," I assert.

"But you think my mom killed him."

I keep my gaze locked on Tessa's, making sure she can see my sincerity when I tell her, "Love killed him. He gave himself up to it, and it completely destroyed him."

"And that's why you can't let yourself be in a relationship."

"I told you that already, Tess."

I can see emotion broiling in her green eyes. She's getting even more upset, despite my attempts to reassure her that even though she's Mary's daughter, I don't blame her for my brother's death.

"Yes, Nathan, you did, and I thought I understood at the time. Now, I really see what you mean." Something in her tone tells me that there's more to her bland tone.

Her voice is almost icy when she spits, "But I suppose you're good with one-night stands and fucks in limos, right?"

I flinch as an inexplicable pang of hurt hits me, but I respond in a lazy drawl, "Is that a problem for you? If I remember correctly, you didn't want a relationship, either."

She's breathing hard now, her lips moist and parted, and my gaze is drawn to the rise and fall of her breasts. As usual, there's an answering tightening in my groin, which I ignore.

"Don't you put this on me, Nathan. You never did have any more to give. And you probably never will."

I never will? That hurts. It shouldn't, though, because remaining single is what I've always wanted. And a woman who understands early on that I can't commit is something I always thought I needed.

"You seem to know a whole lot about my thoughts and intentions, Tess."

She shrugs. "I'm just choosing to believe what you're telling me. But it doesn't matter. You're right, I don't want a relationship with you, either. It would jeopardize everything I've built, so..."

"Exactly. And since we perfectly understand each other, what the fuck are we arguing about, then?"

"Precisely. I don't even see any point in us talking." She motions back and forth between us. "Since we're not even fucking, I mean."

Whoa. Is she trying to get rid of me? "Well said, Tessa. I agree."

"Fabulous!"

We stare at each other, neither one of us wanting to be the first to back down.

I see everything she's not saying in her eyes. She wants more from me, but she doesn't *want* to want more. That's why she's so upset and conflicted.

It just so happens that I want more, too. My mind burns with everything I want to admit but dare not say.

I want to give you more, Tess. So much more. Things I've never thought I'd want to give a woman. My name. My body. My children. My pleasure. My wealth.

My better judgment is screaming at me to take a step back from this insanity because those are the same things Ciaran wanted with Mary.

Instead, I take a literal step forward, and a mental step off the ledge. "Tess—"

"I should go home. I can't be here with you. We'll draw more attention than we already have." She turns to leave, but I grab her arm to stop her.

Her interruption just saved me from blurting out some really crazy things. Things that cannot be unsaid once they're out of my mouth.

I'd be wise to keep my mouth shut, so instead, I say. "No, Tess, you stay. The planning team will miss you if you leave. Not to mention, your hot rockstar *friend*."

She snaps her head back to me, and I know my reference to Chris has annoyed her. I don't care; better to have her angry than staring up at me with those doe eyes that beg me to give up everything.

To do those beautifully decadent things she needs to feel better but won't admit to needing because she wants to remain professional.

"I'll go instead. See you on Tuesday, Tess." The Guardian Angels have requested an audience with senior executives for the initial presentation of the KidStation software, so I'll have no choice but to see her during the meeting.

"See you, then," she replies in a hard tone, but her eyes betray her reluctance to end the conversation.

Pulling open the door and leaving Tess with so much unsaid between us is suddenly the hardest thing I've ever done.

Chapter Fourteen

TESSA

Stay calm, Tessa. Just stay calm. Don't cry.

I repeat those words over and over again for the next two hours, enduring the party because I can't bail on the rest of the planning team and because it'll be rude if I don't wait until Ninth Life finishes so I can thank Chris and the rest of the band again.

After Nathan left, I needed a few minutes to compose myself enough to face everyone with a brave smile. Now, my face hurts with the effort it's taking to keep it there.

And my heart just aches with guilt and regret. Because tonight proved to me that I've done an incredibly stupid thing and fallen in love with Nathan King, the one man who I have no business falling for. A man who must find the idea of love so repugnant.

I can't imagine how much he must hate my mom. Or me. And how much of our relationship might be due to him wanting revenge on my parents for what they did to his brother.

Although he didn't admit it, I don't see how he couldn't hate me. If someone did that to my twin sister, I'd loathe their guts. I'd wish them dead. If their daughter fell in love with me, I'd take my revenge and break her heart, too.

Ciaran might have been the one who had his heart stomped on, but it was Nathan who lived to suffer the pain.

"Girl, you're a miracle worker." Diane comes and throws an arm over my shoulder. "I can't believe Chris Dean and I are actually in the same room! Like, breathing the same air!"

I chuckle, shaking my head at her dramatics. "It's the Chris effect."

"He's so sexy. I almost had to shove a patient out of the way to get a selfie with him. He was all smoldering heat and crackling testosterone. That selfie is totally going into my spank bank."

I push her away playfully. "Geez. Diane, don't make me nauseous."

She turns to me, remembering why I don't share her ardor. "And you actually *know* him! He's practically like your big brother. What's he like as a person, Tessa?"

I shrug. "He's great, I suppose. Very protective—"

She swoons. "Could he be any more perfect?"

"—and he's a wonderful father." I feel as though that last part needs to be spelt out before Diane gets any more ideas besides using that selfie later tonight.

"Father? He's married?" She looks back to where the band is now packing up, and Chris is signing a few more autographs and taking selfies with patients.

"I'm afraid so, Diane. He just keeps his private life away from the media, but yes, he is married. Happily so, might I add."

"And that, Tessa, is the sound of my heart breaking."

I chuckle in spite of my dark mood. "You'll get over it, babe."

"But seriously, this was one awesome party. Maybe we can suggest that they do the same for the kids. I mean, if Dr. King can bring other kids over to the Fount just so they aren't lonely, I'm sure he will agree to throw a party for them."

My stupid heart lurches at the sound of his name. I want him so badly, and I hate the way we left things. I'm scared of him not feeling the same way, and pushing him away is an easier pain to deal with. At least then it's self-inflicted.

"True," I agree, "we should include that as part of our recommendations next month."

"Or you could just ask him, girl. That'll make things happen quicker. You know he'll do anything you ask of him." She winks and cocks her head.

I whirl to face her. "What do you mean?"

"Oh, come on, Tessa, the man is in love with you," she says as if it's the most obvious fact in the world, and I'm an idiot for not knowing it.

"He most definitely isn't—"

"Jackson swears it," she states, like that should settle the matter. "He knew the only way to get Dr. King to attend tonight's event was to get you on the planning committee. And boy, did he attend, looking like sex on a stick. I swear, we had to sweep our collective jaws off the floor."

"There's nothing going on between us," I argue, but even to me, my protest sounds weak.

"Well, there should be. Marta says she's not known him to be interested in anyone in the ten years she's been working here. Check it, Tessa: he's hot as fuck, loaded, and he likes you. I'd totally do him. And he looks like he'd be great in the sack."

I close my eyes against the unbidden memories of that night. *He is unbelievable in the sack.*

I busy myself with stacking up unused cups on a nearby table in a bid to hide my reddening face from Diane. "I'm not throwing away everything I've built for a fling with the boss, thank you very much."

"But that's the best part, Tessa, he's technically not your boss. He's purchasing our services, if you will." She shoots me a smug look, proud of herself for dismantling another one of my arguments.

"Our client, then. It's the same thing." Itching to end the conversation that is threatening to erode my resolve, I find Diane something else to do.

"Diane, why don't you go check on Tim and see how much information he gathered from respondents for KidStation?"

She grumbles goodnaturedly about our chat not being over yet, but she makes a beeline for the KidStation stand at the far corner of the room.

Chris finishes talking to the last fan/patient, then he comes over to me.

I give him a quick hug. "Chris, thanks again for doing this, it means a lot to our patients. Everyone had an amazing time."

We'd offered to pay, but the band decided to do this gig for free, claiming that giving back to people who need a little light in their lives is payment enough.

"Of course. Anytime. But this is a great idea, you know. If Max ever tries this in his hospital, his patients might break their legs just to be able to attend."

I chuckle, but something occurs to me. "Wait a minute. Max, as in Montaigne?" I wonder if he's talking about his friend, the trauma and orthopedic surgeon.

"Oh, yeah. Max is back in LA to set up his hospital, even though he's still with the Pacific Coast Center until he's ready for the big move. Majority of his patients are bungee jumping, skydiving daredevils, and they'd love something like this party. Hell, they might even kick us off stage and do their own gig!"

I stop listening to the rest after he confirms that the guy who has returned to LA is none other than Max Montaigne.

All I can think of is Isa, my best friend and Chris's baby sister, who Max got pregnant before leaving LA a few years ago. Chris has no clue, and neither does Max.

Shit.

Isa's probably having a meltdown right now.

"When did he return, Chris?" I interrupt.

"About a month ago, but I've not seen much of him, to be honest. He's that busy. Anyway, Tessa, we need to take off, okay? Does Isa know that you invited the band here?"

"No, everything happened really fast, so I didn't get a chance to speak to her yet."

He nods in understanding. "So, I won't say anything to her then."

"Okay, Chris, thanks. I'll call her myself tomorrow," I promise.

"Awesome. She's been so busy with exams— you know how she is with those— but she'll be delighted to hear from you, Tessa." He gives me a hug, then turns to leave.

"By the way," Chris says and suddenly turns back, as if just remembering something. "Nathan King?"

I tense, expecting a brotherly warning to stay away from Nathan. "Yeah?"

I already know the man is a walking commitment phobe with baggage the size of the Grand Canyon, so Chris's warning isn't really necessary. "What about him?"

"Go easy on the guy. He's a proud one but... he's crazy about you."

I blink in rapid succession, betraying my surprise. "Excuse me? You figured that out in the two seconds you interacted with him?"

"It was written all over his face. And as a man who has also been in Crazytown for the past four years since I laid eyes on Milly, it takes one to know one. Do you want me to check him out for you?"

I almost laugh. There's nothing to "check."

I'm the one with the insane family dynamic. My father may or may not be indicted in my mother's death, and my mother may have also been responsible for Nathan's brother's death.

It doesn't check out more than that.

"No, it's all good. It's fine. He's just..."

...a friend.

I stop what I'm about to say. Nathan has never been a friend. He's always been so much more to me.

"He's what?" Chris prompts when I trail off.

"Nothing. I... ah, sort of like him a little bit, that's all."

Chris's dramatic gasp of mock surprise is enough to make me want to smack him. "You don't say?"

He laughs when I playfully shove him. "Okay! Fine, I more than like him. It's just that he doesn't do relationships," I admit dejectedly.

Chris shakes his head like he feels bad for Nathan. "Oh, that's what he thinks. What he doesn't have is a chance against a determined Tessa."

I chuckle. "You know, Chris, I'm actually surprised by how agreeable you are about him. I was worried that you were going to punch his lights out when he put his arm around me earlier."

Chris played the overprotective brother role to a tee back when Isa and I were freshmen at UCLA, and I thought that would have carried over when he saw a man my father's age put the moves on me.

"Did you see the size of him? I'm not messing with that!" Chris chuckles.

"Oh, come on, you say that like he's a mammoth or something. He's just about six three or four, same as you."

"No, I'm kidding. But seriously, you're a big girl now, Tessa. I trust you know what's good for you. Besides, I have eyes. No matter what the man thinks about commitment, he likes you a lot. You should give him a chance."

I wonder if Chris would be this understanding about Isa, although something tells me that he wouldn't extend her the same courtesy. I've never met Max, but both Isa and Chris have talked about how big of a manwhore he is.

"I don't know if I have room for a relationship right now, to be honest. I'm all about my finals." I should be, anyway.

"Su-ure," he drags it out into about five syllables, smirking in that annoying way big brothers have perfected. I only shake my head.

"Anyway, it was great seeing you again, Tessa. Now, I know how you can let yourself get sucked into work, but don't you dare leave for Boston without spending time with your LA family first."

"Of course not, I promise!"

Especially not now that I know that Isa's epic squeeze is back in town.

We should have caught up earlier, but finding time between KidStation and Isa's upcoming competency exams has been hard.

After Chris leaves, the planning committee gets to work putting the hall back to its original state. After we're done, I join the carpool that drops Tim, Diane, and me off at the Fount staff quarters.

In less than two minutes of getting into the house, I hear pounding on my front door.

Nathan?

My heart races with excitement as I sprint to the door and throw it open.

I'm speechless with shock with what, or rather who, I see standing there.

Chapter Fifteen

NATHAN

> *May 24th*
>
> *These damn tiny crystals of death keep showing up everywhere. Turbid and glossy, just like grains of couscous. They melt into oblivion in heat and water, and that's when the games truly begin.*
>
> *Lately, I'm no longer strong enough to resist. It's so much easier just to let go and do what Dee says. Whenever Dee calls him, Black comes to me. It's not real, but it's so hard and painful to not believe it.*
>
> *It's all a game. A game of death. You find the crystals before they find you and you win. You don't and you die.*

I STARE UNBLINKING AT the ring binder in front of me until my eyes hurt, but I can't stop.

What the actual fuck?

A thought, too bitter to contemplate, yet an accurate one, begins to unfold in my mind.

I've been reading the journals every night since last week when Vause made me a copy, having realized that I seem to know a lot more about Mary than everyone else.

I am also desperate to find answers, perhaps even more than everyone else.

The detectives were right. Mary deliberately wrote in a way that made it difficult for anyone else except John and Ciaran, and by extension, myself, to figure out what she was talking about.

If John had any idea that she wrote in these things, they would have long been destroyed. He probably thought she was writing her cookbooks.

Two things are certain from the entries. One, she never calls Ciaran by his name, only Black, the nickname I gave to him. Two, Black never speaks to her. Dee does all the talking.

I don't need an astrophysicist's brain to know that Dee is John.

And those fucking crystals.

There have been several mentions of games and death, but this entry is the first time that she talks about the crystals.

I remember going to Ciaran's apartment on the day his body was pulled out of Lake Orange. As usual, the place was in shambles, reflecting the state of my twin brother's mind in the months leading up to his death.

Still numb from shock, I automatically started straightening the place, as if I was expecting Ciaran to show up later that evening.

I swept up what I assumed were grains of couscous in Ciaran's bedroom, thinking nothing of it. Mary had lived a big chunk of her life with her grandparents in Morocco and must have rubbed off on him.

Now, after reading Mary's journal, I realize that what I swept up may not have been the semolina grains. They were crystals. Some kind of drug? Maybe.

Both Ciaran and Mary died under very curious circumstances, and it seems as though both were exposed to the same crystals around the time of their deaths.

Mary seemed to have been well-acquainted with them, like she'd seen them many times before. She was thought to be schizophrenic within the last few months before she died.

Was someone gradually exposing her to them, making it so that she would appear to be mentally unstable?

If John lived in the same house and was not affected, he must have been the one peddling and planting those crystals and also knew how to protect himself against them.

Double fuck.

Could it be from the so-called "lab" that John spent so much of his time at? I need to speak to Tess to confirm my theory.

My chest tightens with excitement at the thought of talking to her again. As awful as arguing with her was, I was still left with a pleasurable buzz afterward just from being around her.

Spending time with her, even if we were arguing, gave me an euphoric high that couldn't be rivaled by any other feeling.

I tell myself that my sudden need to talk to her is because of what I just discovered about the crystals, but really, I would have never lasted the entire weekend without squashing this shit going on between us.

I've never been into a woman this much before, never imagined that my sanity would depend on whether or not we were on good terms.

And because Tess is so damn stubborn, I suspect that she's prepared to hold onto her grudge until Tuesday's presentation, where I'd be tortured to within an inch of my life by being forced to watch her kill it in the conference room.

I, on the other hand, am already feeling like I might burst out of my skin with need.

A couple of months ago, the feeling wasn't this bad, but the craving seems to be growing out of proportion, like a damned weed.

Could this all-consuming need be what Ciaran felt for Mary?

God, I hope not.

Still, I can't stop myself from picking up the phone and dialing her number.

"Hi." She sounds breathless when she answers after a few seconds.

When she says my name, the pleasure that rushes through me, ending in my cock, scares me.

I'm pretty much done for.

"Baby girl."

However, by the end of our conversation, my euphoria has been completely replaced by horror, the likes of which I've never known.

Chapter Sixteen

Tessa

I throw my door open, half-expecting to see Nathan waiting for me on the other side and knowing that I won't be able to resist him tonight.

I just want to stop thinking and… feel. Nathan knows just how to get me out of my head and focus on the here and now.

But it's not Nathan.

It's my father. The one who has never visited me since I left home, not at UCLA or even at Northeastern. And now, he's here, at almost midnight.

What the hell?

"Dad? How do you even know where I live?"

"Oh, come now, you told Joyce. She mentioned that you were staying in the Fount's staff quarters."

I don't recall saying anything like that to Joyce or even telling her about working with the Fount, but then again, I was really upset by that argument with my dad, so the details are patchy.

All I can clearly remember from that night is how I got swept away by Nathan's all-consuming passion. God, I miss him right now.

I give myself a quick mental shake to get rid of the heated memories.

Get it together. Can't be dreaming of another man while your father is standing right in front of you.

I step aside to let him in, not seeing any other way around it. "Dad, to what do I owe this visit?"

He comes in and looks around. Immediately, his eyes snag on the scattered pages on the table.

Detective Warner mentioned that my dad got a binder, too. So even if he never read them like he claimed, he undoubtedly recognizes my mother's journals.

"Don't tell me that you're wasting your time trying to make sense of that load of unmitigated crap."

For some reason, I don't want to antagonize him tonight. I just want to get this visit over with.

"It's gibberish, I'll admit, but the Valencia PD keep asking me if I've read through them so I can help with their investigation."

My response seems to put him more at ease, his shoulders losing their tension, but he still has a judgmental look on his face. "You should have been smarter from the beginning and not gotten involved at all. Anyway, how are you?"

I'm still trying to work out what he's doing here. He needs something, that much I'm sure of, but what? "I'm good. What do you need, Dad?"

"Joyce really wants you at the wedding and somehow thinks that you won't attend because at the engagement party, you left abruptly with Nathan King. "

His tone is deceptively casual, but I know better. He's watching me like a hawk, waiting to dissect every nuance of expression on my face.

The reason John Blackwell is here is because of his last six words.

He wants to know what's going on between Nathan and me—and perhaps to check if I know about Ciaran King, the man he stole my mother from. The man who stole my mother's love back. The man whose twin brother stripped him of his wealth, took his daughter's loyalty from him, and is now possibly sleeping with her.

I can understand his pain and his hatred for Nathan, but he's not some innocent victim.

I decide to go on the offensive. "Is it true, Dad?"

"Is what true?"

"The affair between Ciaran King and Mom?"

He visibly pales, probably because he doesn't expect that I would know about Ciaran, but he recovers quickly. "I'm afraid so, Tessa. Mary was a master pretender. She enjoyed playing games and repeatedly used the man for sex, deceiving him into thinking that she would leave me for him."

"You realize that the detectives would see that as a motive if they found out that she was unfaithful to you?"

A sneer overtakes his face. "I bet that's why King told you about it, the sneaky motherfucker. It's too bad he can't pin me to the crime scene. Has it occurred to you that King himself has a stronger motive to kill your mother than I do?"

"What are you talking about?"

"Mary destroyed his twin brother and caused his suicide. Has anyone thought of asking King where he was at the time of Mary's death?"

I can't say anything to that because it's too ludicrous to imagine. Nathan is not a killer. "If you suspected any foul play in Mom's death, why didn't you say that to the police when it first happened? Why would you be satisfied with them ruling it as an accidental death?"

He shakes his head in disgust. "I keep telling you, Tessa, you're too damn gullible—"

He suddenly breaks off in a coughing and choking fit. "Ex–cuse me," he manages in between coughs.

"Are you okay?" I move closer but resist the urge to thump on his back.

He nods his head, still hacking away. "Water, please."

A knot of concern settles in my gut. Maybe it's because I've been working in a cancer center, but I'm already imagining the worst. I quickly fetch a glass from the kitchen, fill it with water, and bring it back. He takes it gratefully, downing half of it in one gulp.

He eventually settles after another prolonged coughing fit. "It's this damn irritating cough. I can't get rid of it, no matter what I try. It hits out of nowhere, and sometimes, I cough up a bit of blood."

I don't want to care, but I can't help it. He's still my dad, after all. "You should get that checked out. Having a cough that doesn't go away over several weeks isn't a good thing."

"Oh, yes, definitely. I'm seeing someone about it next week."

I debate whether to get him to leave or continue to ask about Mom. My curiosity wins out.

"But why did you pursue Mom in the first place? She was clearly with another man at the time. Was it because Ciaran was dirt poor and worked for your family, so you wanted to prove that you were better?"

A terrible look creeps into his eyes. "That's what his brother told you, isn't it? He sure has a lot to say about your mother, doesn't he?"

I know he's trying to plant seeds of doubt into me. Trying to get me to doubt my reality. It's what he does, but I know all his tricks by now.

"No, Dad, you tell me your own truth. Because it seems like you pursued a woman who was in love with someone else, and then, out of the blue, she's engaged to you. Did your family threaten hers? Blackmail her?"

"I told you, she was playing games. She was never going to marry that lowlife. We were in love from the beginning, but even I couldn't put up with Mary when I realized how thoroughly disturbed she was."

The accounts I've heard from Nathan and my dad don't align, but I know whose story I believe.

"Are you saying that she was playing both of you at the same time? The poor, new girl who'd not long moved to the States from another country?"

He must hear the skepticism in my tone because he says, "You should be careful with whatever Nathan King is feeding you. Mary was your mother. Her death was tragic, no doubt about that. But ultimately, you decide if you want to believe someone with an ax to grind with our family over the cold, hard facts."

"Our family? We've never been a family. You adopted me as a tool to make your wife happy, and when I couldn't fulfill that purpose, you were more than ready to discard me."

"Now, Tessa—" he tries to interject, but I don't let him.

"All those times you tried to justify your affairs, saying that Mom was frigid and emotionless, you never once told me it was because Mom couldn't stop loving another man while married to you."

Throwing his hands in the air, he sends me an incredulous look. "What did you expect me to say? Desecrate your memories of her by telling you what a slut she was?"

I flinch, repulsed by his callous words. "Possibly. You never had anything good to say about her anyway, dead or alive."

Instead of replying, he changes the subject entirely. "Who else do you think has a copy of that journal?"

"Why do you care? It's just a load of crap, isn't it?"

He appears to lose some of his animosity, and his voice softens. "I've told you so many times, Tessa, the Blackwell family is a closed unit. Whatever happens with us stays within the family. We might be at war among ourselves, but we maintain a perfect front so that the generations coming after us have a name they can be proud of."

He takes a step closer to me, his tone earnest. "I'm just trying to protect the Blackwell legacy. Something *you* should be concerned about instead of peddling half-baked speculations from an aggrieved party."

Okay. I'm no longer interested in finding out why he married Mom, I just want him out of my house.

The quickest way to achieve that is to play along. "Okay, I hear you, Dad. As far as I know, no one else has been given the journal. I can't say if the detectives have been speaking to other people, though."

"Good," he says and seems to visibly relax.

"You can tell Joyce that I'll be at the wedding. Otherwise, you can rest easy that I'll cook up a fantastic excuse that she'll believe." I stare pointedly at the door, hoping he gets the message before I need to throw him out.

"Fair enough. Just remember that whatever King tells you, it's more lies than truth," he insists, not showing any intention of leaving yet.

"Okay, I won't listen to his lies anymore."

My phone vibrates in my pocket, and I pull it out to see Nathan's name. A small sigh of relief slips through before I can stop it, then I whirl around, turning my back on my dad to take the call.

"Hi."

"Baby girl."

My heart melts at the sound of his voice, and instantly, my frayed nerves begin to settle. I was angry with him and worried sick after he stormed out that we wouldn't speak for days again, but now, all I feel is joyful relief.

I mute the call for a moment, then throw my dad an apologetic look. "I'm afraid I need to take this, it's from work—and it's the overnight team, too, so I might be a while, okay?" I wait a beat, expecting him to take the cue to leave.

"Oh, go ahead, it's okay." He sits down on the couch and crosses his ankles. "I can always see myself out if you take too long."

I resist the urge to grit my teeth. He always uses this act when he doesn't get his way. He hates being interrupted and always has to have the last word, even if it means waiting for the interruption to stop to do so.

I leave him sitting on the couch, then go through the hallway into my bedroom, lock the door, and sit on the bed. I'm hoping that he leaves before I'm done since I have nothing more to say to him.

I unmute the call. "Hey, Nathan. Everything okay?"

"Yeah. I shouldn't have let us leave things the way we did tonight. We really are beyond walls and masks, don't you agree?" he rumbles, and I have to close my eyes against the tide of pleasure rising in my chest.

"Do you know what I mean?" he presses when I don't say anything.

I do. "We're beyond acting like we don't care." Like what's between us isn't bigger than what either of us can dismiss.

"Absolutely. I know that it was hard to hear about your mom, and perhaps I could have delivered it in a more thoughtful, less jarring way. I'm sorry, Tess."

A giddy smile stretches my lips. "It's okay, Nathan, I appreciate the apology." Hearing him say that he was sorry for the way he handled things is all I wanted, and now that I have, I know that I can move past our argument.

"So, I was frustrated and annoyed tonight, you know," he reveals.

"Why?"

"I was frustrated because I want you, no holds barred. You keep saying that you don't want to be an item, but your eyes, Tess, they tell a different story."

I wonder if he knows that I was on the verge of confessing my feelings to him tonight before I got swept over with guilt when I heard what happened to Ciaran.

What my family did to him.

He continues, "And I was annoyed because you didn't think I had anything to offer you."

I suck in a breath. "I'm sorry. That wasn't a very kind thing to say."

"Not to mention untrue, Tess. I do want to give you more."

My heart starts to pound harder in my chest, anticipating what he might say next. "What are you saying, Nathan?"

"I'm saying that we should probably negotiate how much you're comfortable with because I want to make you mine."

Oh, my God.

I expected he'd say something like this, but I wasn't prepared for him to say it quite like *that*. All growly and sexy.

I desperately try to unglue my tongue from the roof of my mouth while ignoring the fact that my ovaries are going stark raving mad. They have to be, because there's nothing sane about the tightening and fluttering going on in my pelvis.

I press a palm flat against my throbbing stomach.

"Er, Nathan," I begin.

"I understand if you want—or need—space to process everything."

"I don't want space per se..." I say quickly.

"Tell me what you want, then."

You. Deep inside me.

Where the hell did that thought come from? I bite my lip to hold in a whimper.

When I don't respond, he rasps, "Let me start. I want to see you tonight. I really need to hold you. Do you want the same thing?"

How am I already slick with arousal?

"Yes," I whisper. *School finals be damned.*

"Good, I'm coming to you right now. There's something else I need to tell you. It's about the journals. But we don't have to get into that tonight. Tonight, I just want to hear you snore."

I giggle. "Maybe I only snore after I've had my brains fucked out."

"Jesus, Tess. We're on very thin ice here, and you know it."

I smirk at his growly tone. "You're right, I shouldn't be pulling on your achy balls—ahem, legs."

"That's it, you're getting a spanking for teasing an old man."

"I don't know, he'd have to catch me first. I mean, I'd like to see how fast the old man can run when he's rock-hard and leaking pre-cum."

"Theresa Jane Blackwell. You fucking temptress. In exactly twenty minutes, you'll be on your knees with your dirty mouth stuffed full of my cock, and then, I'll have you screaming so loud that the neighbors will hear you."

My mouth waters, and my toes curl in anticipation. Suddenly, I can't wait. I start undoing my jeans, so I can change into something sexy, when I remember my unwanted guest.

Crap. Nathan made me forget where I was for a hot minute.

"Fine," I say with a feigned air of boredom. "You can do all that when you get your hands on me. But I've got company now, so make it an hour. My dad is here, believe it or not."

"Come again?" Every trace of playfulness drains out of his voice.

"He just turned up on my doorstep tonight. He seems unwell, but I suspect he came to talk about you. I think he's just heard something about us, and he wants to be sure that my loyalties don't lie with the Blackwell enemy number one."

When we went to Valencia together last week, I'd been too terrified to go inside the police station right away, so Nathan had pulled me out of the car and against him in a long and intimate hug, right there in the parking lot. That might have gotten tongues wagging all the way back to my dad.

"Is he inside your house now?" Nathan asks.

"Yeah, he's waiting in the living room. Or he might have left in annoyance by now. But I didn't hear the door, so my guess is that he's still on the couch."

"Fuck!"

I hear his curse but don't quite get why he's so riled up. Then again, they hate each other, and with good reason.

"I know, right? It's very much out of the blue, not to mention at such an ungodly time. I have half a mind to throw him out right now."

"Can he see you as we speak?"

"No, I'm in the bedroom. Why?"

"Listen to me, baby. It's important that you stay away from John. Do not let him close enough to touch or speak to you."

"What's going on, Nathan?" Fear seeps into me at how serious and afraid he sounds, like he truly believes that I'm in danger.

"I saw some things in the journals just before I called you. He might be dangerous and no doubt up to something. I'm calling the police right now. Put the phone down and find an excuse to go outside. Do not stay in that house with him, do you understand?"

"Um, yeah, okay."

My mind is racing with possibilities, but before I can launch into questions, he starts to make another call.

I hear him read out my address in a clipped tone into another phone, presumably his landline, while I focus on slowing down my breathing and keeping myself calm.

"Nathan, what did you find in the journals?" I ask as soon as he gets off the other line.

He pauses, and I know he's debating what or how to tell me, which means it's probably bad.

Like committing murder bad.

And the man in question is in my living room.

I run my free hand through my hair, grabbing a fistful of the strands, as Warner's face floats before me. I recall his repeated pleas to read through the entries.

"I'm such an idiot for not reading Mom's journals."

"No, Tess. Even if you read them, you wouldn't have figured it out. That's one of the things I thought we needed to discuss. I just didn't imagine that he'd turn around and target you."

I hear shuffling, then a door shuts in the background. He's leaving his house. "What do I do now?" I whisper, trying not to panic.

"If you can get past him, go into the kitchen, slip through the back door and into the back stairwell. You're only a few floors up, so it's not too far to run down the stairs. Or..."

"Or what?"

"If he's being hostile or you don't think you can get past him, then wait in your room, lock the door, and open the windows."

I weigh my options. The bedroom door is already locked, but I feel far from safe. I don't see how opening the windows will improve my anxiety. "Um... I'll leave. I think I can get past him."

"Good. The police will meet you out front, and I'll be there before you know it. Don't take anything with you, not even a coat. Can you do that for me?"

I don't realize that my entire body has started shaking until I hear my bedframe start to creak.

"Tess?" he prompts.

"Yes, yes, I'll be careful."

"Okay, love, you'll be fine. Go now."

"Love? Surely, that was a slip of tongue, Nathan. You can't possibly mean..."

"Tess, *go*!" he barks.

I jump at his authoritative tone, remembering the situation at hand. "Okay! Geez."

Chapter Seventeen

Tessa

I pull open the door, pausing at the threshold. For an awful moment, I imagine my dad standing right outside the door, listening to my call this whole time, but all I find is air.

Taking a deep breath and exhaling through my nose, I pray that I'm not shaking too hard and that he won't take one look at my ashen face and know everything.

I can do this. He doesn't appear to be armed. He has a terrible hacking cough and even looked ill.

I step back into the living room and find him standing with a hanky pressed to his nose and holding the remainder of his glass of water out away from his body like it might have feces in it.

Something else raises the hairs on my nape. His smile is the cruelest I've ever seen.

I don't have time to process what he's doing, all I feel is the chill running down my spine. Now I know without a shadow of a doubt that he has a sinister agenda tonight.

...if I go and Tessa asks those questions, he'll play those deadly games again.

I may not have read the journals, but I remember that line from the first time Warner told me about reopening the case.

Praying that my voice doesn't betray my terror, I say, "Sorry about that. Work has been quite hectic the past couple of weeks, and now, I've just been asked to deliver a report first thing Monday. I'm going to need some coffee so I can get right to it. Do you want one?"

Without waiting, I start toward the kitchen, but his cold voice stops me.

"Work, huh? You little whore. That was King on the phone, wasn't it? You're going to meet him tonight after I leave, aren't you? You're going to tell him everything we discussed."

I break out in a cold sweat. "I don't know what you're talking about."

"You think I don't know that you're spreading your legs for that shitstain King, just like your mother did. I asked you if anyone else had the journals, and you said no. Well, he's got it, and he plans on using it."

Shit, how does he know? Did the detectives tell him? "I have no idea how he got it," I deny.

He only shakes his head, anger causing his face to turn red and lines to wrinkle his forehead.

"All the while, everyone thought I was the only one cheating. But for eight good years, Black fucked my wife. Way more than I ever did. Even after I killed him, she never stopped wanting him. Dreaming of him. Moaning his name. Imagining I was him whenever I was inside her. Did you know that Ciaran means black?"

I'm rooted to the spot, trying hard to remember what I should do.

Okay, kitchen, backdoor, outside.

I start to back away, slowly, but he follows, still talking all the while.

"And then, you saw Black's identical twin, and you became obsessed with him. You stopped being daddy's girl, and like a bitch in heat, you started panting after a man twice your age. When you gave him a lap dance in full-view of the whole town, I knew then that you and your mother were both possessed with Black's evil. And I knew what I needed to do."

I'm speechless. He saw me that night on the pier? And he waited this long to say anything?

"Only, you ran away, didn't you? Did he tell you to go? What was it that fucker said to make you leave town that night?"

I back away faster, but as if he knows what I might do, he goes around the island in three quick strides and blocks the back door with his body before he starts to advance on me.

"What are you doing?" I ask, my voice high with fear, as he gets even closer to me.

"Something I should have done a long time ago."

Run! I turn back to the living room, hoping to get out through the front door instead.

Before I can fully turn away, however, he just tosses the water remaining in his glass at me. It hits me square in my face.

What the hell! Water sprays up my nose, and a horrible, pungent smell fills the air.

I scrub at my face frantically. "Acid! Oh, my God, Dad, you threw acid on me!"

He starts to laugh maniacally, even as the room feels lighter and begins to wobble.

"Acid would be eating through your flesh by now, my darling, dumb bitch. No, this is much better. It's untraceable. Completely degrades in fifteen minutes. But even more fascinating is the things it makes you want to do. Interestingly bizarre things, like flying down the balcony to meet your waiting lover."

"Oh, God." My vision darkens, and I can no longer see his face, but I still am faintly processing what he's saying.

"Or take a swim in the freezing-cold Lake Orange," he adds. "You, though," he says, and his voice sounds like it's coming from a great distance, like an echo, "you'll want to have a nice, warm, and relaxing soak because you're tense, aren't you?"

As I try to make sense of what's happening, he continues, "It means you won't show up for your booty call tonight, so King will have to come and find his little whore naked and waiting for him. Too bad you won't be breathing anymore."

Suddenly, I want nothing more than to have a bath. But it doesn't make sense to do so right now because I need to leave the apartment, even though I can't remember why.

I fight the feeling for as long as I can, but it's too strong. Resisting that insane desire drains so much energy out of me until I'm left with no more strength.

Finally, after what feels like ages, but it may only have been seconds, I give in to the insane urge. I start to walk out of the kitchen. Immediately, an intense feeling of peace envelopes me, rewarding my capitulation.

Everything appears pitch-black, but the way to my bathroom is lit like a beacon, drawing me closer. I make my way as though moving through molasses, my only thought about how soothing the water will feel around me.

I fill the tub, checking the water temperature. *It has to be warm*, I say to myself.

I can no longer hear my dad's voice behind me, only blissful silence and a deep-seated fulfillment in doing what needs to be done.

I don't want to remove my clothes, as it seems like too much hassle when all I long for is the feel of the warm water surrounding me, but I find myself physically unable to skip that crucial step.

With great effort, I peel off all of my clothes and finally slip into the warm, welcoming depths of the water, feeling the last of my doubts melt away.

I can't wait for him to get here. Nathan's gorgeous face with his slight smirk is the last thing I see before I'm drawn into a peaceful sleep.

Chapter Eighteen

Nathan

The ride to the Fount's staff quarters, a high-rise building with sixteen floors, takes me less than fifteen minutes on my Harley Davidson.

I fly off the bike and at once note that Tess isn't anywhere outside waiting for me.

Where the fuck are the cops? Is John still in there with her?

I forgo the elevator and take the stairs three at a time until I reach the sixth floor. I'm about to kick in her door when it swings open, and a man jumps back in shock and partly to avoid me crashing into him.

It's John Blackwell.

Blood drains from his face when he sees me, and he freezes in shock. I have no such hesitation. I grab him by the neckline of his shirt, looking around the apartment for Tess.

"Where is she?" I drag him with me as I take a few steps into the living room. "Tess?" I yell.

There's no response.

"Where the hell is she, asshole?"

"You think I don't know that you're fucking my daughter?" is his only reply.

I tighten my grip on his neck and slam him into the wall with enough force to make his teeth rattle while I search him for any weapons he might want to defend himself with. "I asked you a fucking question!"

"She stepped outside to take a call," John replies calmly.

I look toward the front door, about to drag him there when he gestures in the other direction.

"Not that way, she went through the door in the kitchen, over there."

I drag him into the kitchen, throw him against the counter, and go to pull the back door open while he calls me a few choice names and rubs at the skin of his neck.

"Tess?" I call.

Silence.

Has she gone around the building to the front, then?

Out of the corner of my eye, I see John move toward the sink and dry heaves over and over. He spits, then turns the water on. Still, I watch him like a hawk, waiting for him to finish throwing up so that I can resume my chokehold on him.

As if the dry heaves aren't a dead give away, something about his rigid posture is wrong and raises alarm bells. His muscles are tensing and locking together.

Thinking that he's about to attack with a weapon, I mentally prepare for his strike, but I'm also curious to see what he thinks he can do to me. I've got over a hundred pounds on him, and a decent amount of that is muscle.

I pretend to look outside for any trace of Tess, but I notice the moment he slips a hand inside his back pocket and digs out a small bag of grainy material.

I know exactly what it is, and I see red.

I'm on him in a flash, shoving him away from the sink, my fist connecting with his nose. I feel a crunch as the cartilage gives way, and blood spurts out his nostrils.

"You sonofabitch. That's it, isn't it? Whatever the fuck it is you used to kill your wife and my brother in cold blood."

He doesn't see me. He's not cowering or even holding onto his broken nose. Nor does he care that his cover is blown. All he seems to be preoccupied with is throwing that pack inside the sink of running water.

... *They melt into oblivion in heat and water, and that's when the games truly begin.*

What the hell?

If there was any doubt as to his motives for being here, that action just erases it.

I drag him out of the kitchen, out of the reach of water and into the hallway, and then, I let my fists loose on him.

My initial plan is to incapacitate him, but now, beating him to a pulp feels too satisfying to stop. I feel two of his incisors cut into my fist before they loosen and cave in.

Still, I'm unable to make myself stop, and I start praying for the cops to show up before I kill the man.

Because all I see when I look at him is my twin brother's frozen body in a wetsuit.

The sound of a loud, wet gurgle makes me stop long enough to listen. I can also hear that the bathroom tap is on as water flows steadily.

"Tess?"

John turns his head and spits out a tooth and a wad of bloody phlegm. "I suggested that she wait for you naked like the slut that she is, in a tub full of water."

She's been in there the whole time?

I push myself off of John and run in the direction of the bathroom, my heart in my throat.

I've seen a lot of awful things, but the sight that greets my eyes breaks me open.

The woman I love, submerged in a tub as though sleeping, the water above her beautiful face as still as the surface of a mirror. Her face looks peaceful, soft, while the rest of her body is limp.

No!

The rest of what happens is a blur.

I don't remember carrying her out or laying her on the floor and starting CPR. Or the police crashing in minutes after that.

I don't remember refusing to allow anyone else to take over her resuscitation or hitting the man who tried to drag me off her.

Not until the fog starts to lift from my brain do I realize that the officer I punched was Alvin Ling, a policeman and Marta, my employee's husband.

Chapter Nineteen

NATHAN

I'm hunched over the large window, staring out into the moonless night at the Pacific Coast Trauma Center waiting room when I feel a heavy hand on my shoulder.

I turn to see it's Alvin Ling, with two other officers flanking him.

"Hold out your arms, Dr. King."

"Are you going to put me in handcuffs, Alvin?" I ask.

His eyes twinkle, even though his right one is beginning to swell. "No, you're already in handcuffs. I'm taking them off you, provided you won't hit anyone else."

I look down to see that my wrists are, indeed, shackled, something else I have no recollection of. "No, I won't."

"Good. You're a big man. You can't go around throwing punches. Mr. Blackwell is currently in surgery for the face you rearranged." Somehow, the officers don't look too devastated by that fact.

"And while you should damn well be, you're unlikely going to end up getting charged for this." Alvin points to his evolving blackeye. "I believe you will, at the very least, be hearing from my Marta on this matter, though."

He and the other two officers chuckle, and I look around the room, wondering what on earth could possibly be funny.

Alvin's partner says, "Once you're more settled, Dr. King, we'll need your statement, an account of what you saw and did tonight."

"Sure," I say. Maybe I should have been more worried about what that will entail, but right now, all I can think about is Tess. "What's the latest on Tess?"

Again, I'm not sure how much time has passed between me finding her lying still and peaceful under that water and since she was wheeled into the intensive care unit. What I do know is that every single minute I've spent waiting for updates has felt like an entire year.

"They're doing everything they can for her, Dr. King. I'm sure she'll pull through." Alvin uncuffs me, then returns my wristwatch, and they leave.

I go back to staring unseeingly into the black night, regret eating away at me.

I can't lose her now. We've barely had any time together.

We could have had five years if I'd listened to my gut feeling.

The night that Tessa first came on to me, I was sitting in front of Lake Orange where Ciaran drowned, nursing my anger and resentment for John and Mary.

Something tells me that if I hadn't taken out my grief on Tessa, if I'd listened to her or even relished her need and desire for me, if I had gotten to know the sweet, sexy, and tenacious woman, we would have spent the last five years together.

She would be Tessa King, and far from John Blackwell's reach.

Fuck.

Perhaps if I'd checked the entire house and found her earlier, she might have stood a better chance...

"Dr. King?" a familiar voice calls, and I turn to see Jackson and Gary approaching in matching goofy sweaters and vinyl pants. In spite of my black mood, my mouth involuntarily twitches, and I fight the urge to roll my eyes.

Jackson sees the look on my face and has the grace to blush.

"We were out on the town," he says, like it should explain why they look like a pair of rainbows.

"Even after tonight's rem party?" It seems like ages ago since Tess and I argued and I left the party.

"Don't give us the judgy attitude. Part of this is your fault, Dr. King. We always match to celebrate the Friday nights that we're both off work. Which, I might add, is a rare occurrence."

I grunt. "Work hazard, I'm afraid. But thank you guys for interrupting your circus plans." The corner of my lips lifts in a small smile.

"Heard anything yet?" Gary asks.

"No, still waiting." Patients who have nearly drowned can be so goddamn difficult to resuscitate. A part of me is glad not to have heard from her medical team yet. It means they're still fighting to save her.

I'm dreading the moment a doctor will come in here with the slumped shoulders and slow walk that means... I mentally shake the thought off, grinding my molars to stave off another flash of pain.

Jackson, who had been watching me and no doubt reading the emotions on my face, suddenly holds out his arms. "Come here." Instead of waiting for me to act, he wraps his gangly arms round my bulk while Gary pats my back repeatedly.

I throw my arms around them both, surprised by how much comfort I derive from that simple gesture. It will have to go down in history as one of the best group hugs I've ever received.

"Does Caitlin know?" Jackson asks, referring to my mom, who is currently out of the country.

"About Tess? Why would she?"

"Oh, don't get it twisted, Dr. King, she already knows that you're in love. I've filled her in since you've had no clue what hit you after Tessa came to work with us."

I rear back, disentangling from them. "Tell me you didn't fucking tell her that?"

I wouldn't put it past my easily excitable mother to begin planning for a wedding the moment she sees me talking to a woman.

Because she's never seen it happen. Not since before Ciaran died.

"Dr. King," Jackson states patiently, as though explaining a tough concept to a child, "I could never hide anything from Caitlin, especially not something like this. Bless her, the woman has practically given up on you producing an heir, so she's thinking of doing it herself! I needed to put her out of her misery."

Gary nudges him. "Jack, he's not supposed to know that she told us about the baby thing!"

"Oops." He doesn't look the least bit sorry. "Well, all that is in the past since she's not trying anymore, so we're good."

For fuck's sake.

"Anyhoo. So, does Caitlin know what happened tonight?" Jackson asks me again.

Giving him a deadpan stare, I say in a dry tone, "Why, I have no doubt you'll fill her in."

"I mean, she's far away in Paris, so no need to trouble her for now. We'll tell her once Tessa is better. And Tessa will be right as rain in no time, don't you worry." Jackson places a comforting hand on my shoulder.

I only shake my head, knowing that I have zero control on what news circulates between these two and my mom, so there's no point in asking them not to say anything. "How did you even hear about everything?"

"Marta called us," Gary replies. "She sends her prayers to Tessa. She also says she won't be speaking to you because of Alvin's black eye. And you know she's the queen of death by silent treatment."

"Fuck, don't I know it." Marta Ling will exact her pound of flesh for me punching her husband. Granted, I didn't know it was him at the time, but she'll still make me work for her forgiveness.

Perhaps a peace offering of flowers, chocolates, and a paid leave might be a decent start to trying to get the head of my treatment unit fully back on my side.

Jackson and Gary sit and start playing cards they got from the nurses' station to keep themselves from going crazy with worry. I just go back to staring outside into the bleak night, losing myself once again to my thoughts.

Tess needs to make it. There are so many things I want to show her. Tell her. Do with her.

After about another hour of waiting for news on Tessa's condition, Chris from Ninth Life shows up, followed by two women.

I don't even bother to ask how he knew to come, putting nothing past those two clowns playing cards in the corner.

He comes straight to me, and without saying a word, pulls me into a hug. I gratefully accept his embrace, patting him on the back, too.

"You came?" I check the time to see that it's 2 a.m.

"Of course, as soon as I heard. I live about fifteen minutes away from here."

He puts his arm around the tall, pretty blonde beside him. "Meet my wife, Milly. Darling, this is Nathan King, Tessa's friend and CMD of the Fount."

I take her hand, barely able to mask my shock and relief that he has no interest whatsoever in Tess.

Chris smirks at my reaction, and I'm sure he knows what I'm thinking. Thankfully, he chooses to introduce the other woman he came in with instead of calling me out. "And this is my sister, Isabel."

"Hi, Nathan." Isabel's grasp is surprisingly firm when I shake her hand, and even though I can see that she's been crying, there's a wicked twinkle in her eyes and a knowing smile on her lips. She knows me.

I don't remember ever treating her, and I don't sleep around, so there's no chance of that, either.

"I'm a first-year surgical resident here. Tessa and I have been friends since our pre-med year at UCLA."

"That's wonderful," I say, "it's very nice to meet you."

And at once, I realize how she must know me. If they shared their teenage fantasies, then Tess most likely told her about me.

I look from Chris to Milly and back at Isabel. These people are more than Tess's friends. They are her family. I can tell that much from how concerned they appear and how quickly they came once they found out.

"Do we know how it happened?" Chris asks.

A hard look enters my eyes. "It was an accident." He looks down at my bleeding knuckles, then back up at me. He says nothing and just nods. "We'll wait with you." He leads the women over to a few chairs to sit down, then gets them water.

Tim and Diane are next to arrive—again, no doubt thanks to Jackson and Gary—and in another hour, the emergency room staff very kindly offers our growing group a private waiting room.

I wouldn't have minded staying where we were, but Jackson already accepts on behalf of everyone. They didn't want our presence at the ER to become social media fodder since Chris and I are considered celebrities.

I can't even scoff at that. The last thing I need is Tess's privacy invaded by meddling fans and money-hungry lurkers.

By four in the morning, sandwiches and coffee are being passed around. I don't eat or drink anything, my stomach in tight knots over how long it's taking to get her stabilized.

I clench my fists, refusing to imagine that the ER team still hasn't brought her back yet. The smarting in my knuckles reminds me of something else that I've blocked out of my mind.

John Blackwell.

It's because of me that she got hurt in the first place.

If she didn't come to work for me, she'd be far away in Boston, making waves for Guardian Angels elsewhere. With how brilliant she is, I have no doubt that she would have received multiple other opportunities to lead a campaign.

But she had returned to destroy the brick wall I'd built around my heart. To show me once again that I was wrong about love being a deadly poison.

"Tessa Blackwell's group?" A tall, handsome man in scrubs comes into our private room. I know he's the doctor because he introduced himself to me several hours ago, only I didn't register him at the time. I straighten from the window sill I've been leaning against.

"Yes?" I rush to respond.

He acknowledges everyone but makes a beeline toward me. My heart already lurches with hope at his tired, but confident stride. "Dr. King—"

"Nathan," I correct.

"Nathan. I'm Max. Trauma attending."

Max Montaigne. I remember now. Son of the renowned neurosurgeon, Louis Montaigne. "Talk to me, Max."

"As you know, she suffered a cardiac arrest, and she was touch and go for a while. Bottom line, though, she's recovered now."

"Thank God!"

There's a chorus of relieved sighs in the room.

Max continues, his face growing serious. "Now, she's not out of the woods yet. She will remain in the ICU for now. The good news is she wasn't down for very long, and she was submerged in warm water. Plus, she got high-quality CPR before the ambulance got there."

"Okay," I say, waiting for the other shoe to drop. I've been a doctor for too long and can recognize when there's a dash of bad news to go along with the good.

"We've had to start therapeutic cooling just to be on the safe side, and we won't start rewarming her for another few hours.

But she's in great hands, Nathan, and I'll do my best to see that she's back in your arms in no time."

I raise an eyebrow, wondering what that last part was all about.

"Oh, you don't remember?" He chuckles. "I tried speaking to you earlier, and all you kept saying was how she's the love of your life and you want her back."

I see. The old me would have felt embarrassed, but now, all I care about is Tessa's well-being.

Seeing that there's no use in denying it, I nod. "I was a little delirious, but it's true."

"It's understandable, considering the situation. But she'll pull through," he reassures me.

Then, he turns around to face everyone else and says a little louder for the group, "So, if you want to go home and come back later, we'll hold the room for you."

"No, that's okay, Dr. Montaigne," Jackson replies. "We're all staying here. No one's leaving."

"Come on, Jack, you can't speak for everyone," Gary protests.

"Well, is anyone bailing?" Jackson looks from one face to another, almost daring anyone to contradict him.

"You're such an ass, Jack." Gary gently pushes him backward. "Here's what we'll do. We can take turns going home to refresh."

"I should imagine—" Jackson argues, but I wave my hand to stop him.

"Alright, guys," I interject before they get into an actual argument. "The room is ours. Tess is going to be fine, she's just not up to seeing anyone yet. I love that you're here for us both, but please, go get a bit of rest and return later."

I look everyone in the face, letting them see my genuine gratitude for them staying at my side for as long as they have.

I turn back to let Max know that we'll sort ourselves out, but I find him, Milly, and Chris huddled together in a group hug.

Max's arms are thrown over each person's shoulder, and I realize that the Deans must be related to him somehow. That's how they knew Tess was here.

Only Isabel remains apart from them, sitting stiffly by herself, but I note how furiously she blushes as Max sends her scorching glances over Milly and Chris's heads, even while updating the couple about Tess's condition.

Isabel is the one Max would rather be holding. Chris's baby sister and one of his residents at work. Fucking hell.

And when the hell did I start noticing these things? Marta always said how two people could literally be humping each other right before my eyes and I wouldn't have a clue what they were doing.

Looks like I've just hopped onto the bandwagon of people like Marta—and Jackson, Gary and the rest of the crazy-in-love crew.

I smile ruefully. I'm all in now. I want Tess with me. All of her, in exchange for all of me, for a very long time.

I know she likes me a lot and she finds me attractive, but that doesn't mean she'll be ready for the same thing.

One can never tell with Tess Blackwell.

I return to my spot by the window and stare out into the night, waiting for the dawn of a new day.

Chapter Twenty

NATHAN

It's ten in the morning on Sunday before the sun rises again in my world.

I'm still by the window, but instead of staring blankly at nothing, I'm leaning against the sill, observing the group which has only grown larger since everyone has heard that Tess is likely going to be out of intensive care today if all goes well.

Our small waiting room is overrun with flowers, cards, and get-well-soon balloons.

Everyone is having another round of sandwiches and coffee. There's been so much food consumed here that it's obvious people are comfort-eating. I, on the other hand, can't eat. I'm only drinking water. Lots of it.

Isabel is munching on her fourth chocolate bar this morning.

Between worrying for Tess and trying, and failing, to mask the thermonuclear chemistry between her and Max, whose frequent visits may have more to do with gawking at her than actually giving me updates, she keeps nibbling on snacks to keep her mind occupied.

Even Jackson has picked up on the tense energy between Isabel and Max, but one warning glare from me and he got the message to keep his mouth shut.

I don't understand how Chris and Milly are still oblivious, though.

The entire LA Guardian Angels team and a few from the Boston team are here. Walter Heche, Tessa's director, flew in from Boston this morning, as well Zara, her friend from work.

Jackson has just announced that he would be sending home the crowd of employees and well-wishers from the Fount, which, of course, leads to an argument with Gary.

"I don't see how that's right. People love Tess and have a right to support their boss," Gary protests.

Jackson snorts. "Yes, and I suppose they also get to watch firsthand as Dr. King loses his marbles over a girl after more than a decade of waiting for it to happen, *and* then snag a selfie with Chris Dean while they're at it?"

"Hell no," he continues, "they can drop the flowers off at the floor's reception desk, and Dr. King will personally extend his thanks to them once Tess is better. Won't you, Doc?"

"'Lose my marbles,' did you say?" I suppose by now, the news that I'm in love with Tess has made its rounds at the Fount, considering I was shouting that fact at Max two days ago, and as if Jackson's words weren't proof enough, almost half of the cards are actually addressed to me, not Tess. But I'm sure I've pretty much kept it together since then.

"It's true, Dr. King. Tess got hurt, and you stopped eating and sleeping, yet you're dressed to the nines, freshening up every ten seconds like a prom date waiting for his girl to come down the stairs."

I look down at my simple, gray, form-hugging sweater and black pants, wondering how exactly I'm dressed to the nines. "What's wrong with my outfit?"

As if on cue, a young, smartly-dressed nurse comes into the room. "Ms. Blackwell's group?"

"Yeah." I straighten from the window to address her.

"Tessa is awake."

The noise is deafening. There's screaming, shouting, hooting, and Isabel actually bursts into tears. I simply release a pent-up breath and wait for the nurse to say more.

"She wants her boyfriend."

I blink in shock, but the room again erupts into even louder hoots, and then, I feel Jackson and Gary patting my back.

I'm unable to speak for a few seconds. I never, ever blush. But this gang of friends here are making me feel like a boy with his first crush.

The nurse looks at me. "Are you Nathan?"

"He is, he is!" they yell simultaneously.

Fuck. Joy washes over me as it becomes undoubtedly clear that I'm the one Tess wants. Along with it also comes a pang of worry.

If Tessa thinks I'm her boyfriend, does that mean she's suffered some form of amnesia? Brain damage? Or did she think that calling me her boyfriend would make it more likely for me to be allowed to see her?

I follow the nurse into the elevator and down the corridor until we get to Tess's room.

With every step I take closer to her, I'm determined not to walk away without Tess in my life.

Chapter Twenty-One

TESSA

EVERYTHING IS SO BRIGHT that it makes my eyes hurt, but I can't see anything. My eyes dart around to try to make out any details, but I still can't even see the lights blinding me, just feel them heating my face.

I try to lift my hand to shield my eyes, but it feels too heavy. Someone turns the lights even brighter, and I open my mouth to protest.

Shut it off!

The only sound that comes out is a pitiful croak.

The shadows move around, and I hear a soft voice ask, "Tessa, can you open your eyes?"

Oh, yes. My eyes are closed, that's why I can't see anything. I crack my eyelids open with difficulty but promptly shut them when it feels too intense and shake my head. At once, the lights go dim, and the pressure in my eyes lessens.

"Do you want to try again now?"

I do so, and while my vision is blurry, I can still make out the silhouette of a young woman. She's holding a straw to my mouth.

She must be an angel, surely. How else could she have known that I was so thirsty?

After draining almost the whole cup, she puts it aside and smooths my hair back from my forehead. "I'm Fran, your nurse. How are you feeling?"

"Tired," I croak. "Achy."

Everything feels too heavy, as if someone put a comforter made of cement on top of me. I look around the room and then at myself. I'm in a hospital room. That much I can tell, but why I'm here, I'm not sure.

"That's expected. You're in a hospital, and you've been out for almost two days. The doctor said you can eat, so I'll get you something light, like soup. After that, you can have some Tylenol to help with the pain if you want."

Confused, I wrack my brain to remember how I got here. When I come up empty, I decide to ask, "How did I—"

And then, it hits me.

I was soaking in the tub while waiting for my boyfriend to come. He'd promised to…oh, God. Heat envelopes my face as my nipples bead beneath the thin hospital gown.

Theresa Jane Blackwell. In exactly twenty minutes, you'll be on your knees with your dirty mouth stuffed full of my cock, and then, I'll have you screaming so loud that the neighbors will hear you.

Nathan.

"I'll get your food, okay?" The nurse pats my shoulder and goes to leave, but I grab hold of her hand with surprising strength. Fran's round face comes back into focus, her brown eyes soft with concern.

"I-I...can I see my boyfriend, please?" I ask.

Her brows furrow, and she opens her mouth, I assume to ask me who I mean, when I clarify, "His name is Nathan."

"I can go and get him for you, but first, have some soup. You must be hungry. Then, we'll get you freshened up."

Ravenous, actually, and not for food. The thought of waiting to see Nathan causes my stomach to protest in a different way. "No, I want to see him now."

She pauses and takes a good look at me, and I think my face gets even hotter the more she observes me. I wonder how many of her comatose patients wake up with a different kind of hunger plaguing them.

"Okay," she says with a little smile and glances at the clock on the opposite wall. "I'll check if he's around."

"What day is it?" Not that it matters, I know he'll be here.

"It's 10:50 on a Sunday morning."

It's after she leaves that it occurs to me to worry about my appearance. If I was out for a couple of days, I probably look like death warmed over. I can't let Nathan see me like this.

This time, it takes all my strength to raise my hands to my hair in an attempt to smooth it over. What I find makes my heart sink. It feels like clumps of straw glued together, and I just know that it'll take a decent amount of conditioner to detangle the clumps.

Goodness. How must I look? No wonder she suggested I freshen up first. It's too late to call Nurse Fran back, though.

I cup my hands in front of my face and exhale. There's a faint smell of mint. I send a silent thanks to my nursing team for at least taking care of one aspect of my hygiene.

Before I can freak out further, Nathan appears at the door.

My mouth dries, and I immediately forget everything except how much I've missed him and how good he looks.

He stands just inside the door and leans on the frame, watching me from across the room.

"Tess?"

"Nathan," I say with a sigh, holding out a hand to him.

He slowly approaches my bedside, and as he gets closer, the beeping from the heart monitor behind me gets louder and faster. It soon becomes clear to everyone and their dog how much the man is affecting me.

He smirks as he leans over me. His large palm cradles my head while his other hand holds my mine in a tight, affectionate grip. I love the way his eyes are drinking me in. Like I'm the most beautiful thing he's ever seen.

"You are a sight for sore eyes, baby girl." He presses a kiss to my forehead, then deliberately reaches up to shut off the heart rate machine, which is now beeping like it's about to explode.

"You—I..." I give up on words, instead reaching up to curl my hand behind his head and pull him to me. The moment his mouth covers mine, I want to sob in relief and pleasure. His smell and taste settle into my pores as I cling to him and kiss him like I never want to stop.

My hand strokes down his chest and abs, feeling the delectable ridges of muscles. Has he always been this ripped? I find the hem of his sweater and pull it up so I can reach underneath it and caress the warm skin under there.

Nathan kisses a path to my ear. "Tess, how are you feeling?"

"Hungry. I want you. I feel like I haven't been with you in weeks."

He chuckles. "That's true, actually. It's been a while."

"But why?" Seems like a stupid decision to me, one I can't fathom making.

"You wanted it that way. Until a couple of days ago, that is."

"What am I, crazy?" I can't imagine why I'd have a boyfriend who looks like *this* and not want him railing me at every possible chance.

My expression of disbelief makes him chuckle more. "How much do you remember, Tess?"

"About?"

He huffs out a breath. "For starters, where do you work?"

"Boston. I do charity work with Guardian Angels in Boston, and I have to go back to school for my final semester."

"Okay…" He seems puzzled by my answer, but he fills in some blanks.

"So, you were transferred to the Fount. That's my group of hospitals, and that's how we reconnected. You've been working with me for a couple of months now."

"I thought we'd been together for longer?" Though I meant it as a statement, it comes out sounding like a question.

"It feels that way," he agrees. "We've known each other for a long time. What else do you remember about us?"

Bits and pieces come back to me in quick flashes, enough for me to get the general idea, but not enough to recall the specifics of our relationship.

"I've had a crush on you for a long time. I gave you a lap dance sometime, I think. You loved it."

"True. And about me being your boyfriend, what do you remember about that?"

I shrug. "I mean, the last thing I remember was you threatening to come…and…fuck me until I scream." My voice lowers. "And how much I was looking forward to it."

"Holy hell, woman!" He drops his forehead to my breasts, making me suppress a needy moan.

"I kinda assumed we were a thing... are we not?" My voice doesn't hide how vulnerable I'm feeling. What if he says no? What if I'm just making a giant fool of myself?

Luckily, he doesn't hesitate to reassure me. "Yes, we most certainly are, baby."

"So, what happened to me? The last thing I remember was waiting for you in the bath."

He lifts his head to look at me, and I can see the emotions rolling in the blue depths. "You...dropped off to sleep in the bath and nearly drowned."

Something in his body language tells me that there's more to that story, but before I can pursue it, there's a knock on the door. Someone I assume to be the doctor comes in with Nurse Fran.

Nathan gives them enough room to assess me but doesn't go far or let go of my hand. I'm gripping his just as firmly, too.

The doctor introduces himself as Max Montaigne, and I answer his questions about pain, my breathing, my last menstrual period, and what I remember about being in the bathtub. Then, he listens to my heart and lungs and checks the charts while I watch his every move like a hawk, wondering if I can tell what kind of man he is.

"Any questions for me, Tessa?" he asks.

Do you have any idea how much you hurt Isa when you left? The question pops into my head out of nowhere, but I know that it's an important one.

Still, I don't bother bringing it up. It's not the time or the place. "No," I say instead.

"Okay, we need to talk some more, but only when you're feeling stronger, okay?"

I nod. "Thanks, Doctor."

Nathan joins the conversation. "Max, when can I take her home?"

I love the sound of that. I'm pretty sure we don't live together yet, but he makes it sound like we're one unit. The idea of it makes me want to smile.

"We'd like to keep an eye on her vitals and check her blood work for another day or so, but if everything looks good and Tessa's feeling up to it, tomorrow or the next day would be a good bet. Alright?"

"Sounds good, thank you, Max," Nathan says, reaching out to shake the doctor's hand.

Max smiles at us both brightly, then continues on his rounds.

"So, you need to eat, baby," Nathan says after Max leaves. "Should we do that now?"

"Okay. I could eat."

Nathan gestures to Fran, who nods and leaves the room, presumably to get the food.

"And you have about twenty people waiting to see you if you're feeling up to it," Nathan says.

"Twenty! Who all is out there?"

He starts listing names and ticking them off on his fingers. "Well, the regular Fount folk, but you also have Walter Heche, Betty, and Zara all the way from Boston. Chris, Isabel, and a few of your friends from your pre-med days, just to name a few."

"You're kidding!"

"No, Tess, they're very excited to see you again. There's also someone else who can't wait to meet you."

"Who is it?"

"My mother."

"Your mother!" I almost yell.

He smirks and offers my hand an encouraging squeeze. "You two have never met, she's mostly been away in Europe, but she's been dreaming about meeting my woman for ages, so you'll have to pardon her if she seems overeager. I couldn't get her to wait for a better time."

"Oh, it's okay." I smile. "I'd love to meet your mom, Nathan."

He takes my lips again and kisses me until I'm wet and throbbing. "Nathan—"

Fran interrupts by returning with some soup and bread, effectively putting an end to the plea I was about to make to Nathan to get me off.

He feeds me, despite my insisting that I can do it myself.

After getting washed and dressed, I ask to meet Nathan's mom first. Nathan only lets her stay for about five minutes, but it's more than enough to fall in love with Caitlin's effusive presence. From her soft, welcoming smile and the way her blue eyes go moist, it seems the feeling is mutual.

After Caitlin leaves, Nathan lets in the rest of the crowd, as well as brings in the rest of the flowers and cards that hadn't made it in here before, then stands off to the side to let me see my friends.

He never goes far and keeps looking at me in that loving way of his, but I still catch glimpses of something dark and haunted in his gaze.

I know it's something floating just beyond my consciousness, and I have a feeling that if I focus hard enough, I'm sure I could recall what it is. But all the people talking and laughing around me makes it difficult. I'm sure it'll come to me soon enough, though.

As Isa chats away, I lift my head and catch Nathan doing what I would define as fussing, something I'd never have guessed how much of a turn on it could be.

My eyes follow him as, for what must be the tenth time, Nathan resets the room's temperature, fiddles with the settings of my drip machine, and remotely controls the blood pressure cuff around my arm and the IPC device squeezing at my calves at the foot of the bed.

Max says we could go home tomorrow, but with the constant tightening in my pelvis and how damp my thighs are now, I wonder if I'd be able to wait that long. It feels like it's been a year since I last had Nathan.

He returns to his spot by the door, where he continues talking with Chris. Suddenly, as though he can sense my gaze on him, he turns to look at me. I deliberately let my eyes rake over him, then bite my bottom lip in a way that I hope tells him how horny I am.

He gets it, sends me a sexy smirk, and mouths, "I know, baby. Soon."

My toes curl in anticipation, even as he resumes his conversation with Chris, seemingly without breaking stride.

I cannot wait to get him alone.

Chapter Twenty-Two

TESSA

It takes another couple of days before I get my wish.

In these two days, I've come to understand that my near drowning wasn't an accident. The police have come by the hospital a number of times, but Nathan keeps turning them back or speaking to them himself.

I'm so close to recalling all the details, but everytime I push my mind harder, I get a splitting headache and an inexplicable sense of doom.

I know it must be something very bad.

Yet, I'm surrounded by so much good. A loving boyfriend, supportive friends and coworkers. Nathan's mom, who visits me everyday.

And early this morning, just before Nathan arrived to take me home, Max told me something that I've decided to keep to myself until I remember more.

I cradle my still flat belly, giddy with excitement and nursing a secret smile on my lips.

Now, we're in an Audi A8 I don't recognize as one of Nathan's, speeding toward his Hollywood Hills home.

Although there's a lot I still don't remember—nothing about my childhood, parents, or high school—the moment we enter the gated driveway, flanked on either side by manicured lawns, I know without a doubt that I've never been here before.

But that doesn't make sense, not if I'm dating Nathan. I mean, what girlfriend hasn't seen where her boyfriend lives? "You're not really my boyfriend, are you?"

Hesitating to answer, he shoots me a look as if to decide if he thinks I can handle the truth. Finally, he admits, "Not yet. But we were working our way there. Why do you ask?"

I remain silent, unsure how to process the news.

"I want you, I just want you to have your full memory back so you can decide if you want the same thing."

"Is there a reason I wouldn't want to?"

"Not really, no. It's just because once you're mine, Tess, there's no turning back. Ever."

I like the sound of that. "But what if I never regain my memory?"

"You will. Tess, what you have is dissociative amnesia. The emotional and psychological trauma you experienced triggered your mind to block out those deeply disturbing memories. But there are enough clues still in your life that one of them is very likely going to trigger you to remember everything."

I nod, rooted to the spot as he gets out and rounds the car to my side. Just the thought of regaining my memory sends a bolt of panic through me. Whatever it is must be bad, and it might change my life, so I'd rather live in the moment.

He pulls me into the house. The interior looks even better than the outside, but I don't bother to take it all in because, suddenly, I have him exactly where I want him.

"Nathan," I murmur, snaking my arms around his neck and playing with the silky hair on his nape.

He nuzzles my skin, gently biting down on the skin of my neck and making me shiver involuntarily. "Yes, baby?"

I set to work on the buttons of his crisp shirt. "I want to be with you, no matter what."

"Duly noted." His mouth descends on mine in a hungry kiss while I work feverishly to peel him out of his shirt.

Running my eager hands all over his silky chest hair and muscles and feeling them twitch in response to my touch gives me a shot of feminine pride unlike anything I've ever known.

When we come up for air, he rasps, "Any more serious requests before I lose all higher functions and rational thought?"

"Just one. I seriously need to come, like right now."

"That sounds reasonable." He picks me up in his arms and takes me to the sofa, but instead of laying me across the cushions as I was expecting, he bends me over the high back. My ass is up at the perfect height for his crotch, but my feet aren't touching the floor.

Oh, shit. I don't remember ever taking it this way. Is this the kind of sex we have?

He fists the back of my hospital-issued cotton T-shirt and tears it clean into two, then places his naked chest against my back as he folds over me.

"Ahh... Nathan." That initial contact of his warm, sweet-scented skin on mine feels so unbelievably good. I want more.

He reaches beneath me and palms both my breasts, gently pinching my nipples, and my moans get louder.

He rains open-mouthed kisses and nibbles across my back, and in less than a minute, I start to grind my butt back onto him, seeking his hard length.

"Nathan, please, it's been too long. I want you inside me."

"Will you be a good girl and take it hard?"

Will I? "Yes," I say while panting. "Please, please."

He undoes my jeans and pulls them off me, taking my panties with them. Then, he palms and gently kneads my ass.

"You have the most gorgeous ass, baby." He spreads my cheeks apart and swears at what he finds.

I know it's because of how soaked I am.

"Fuck, Tessa, you're dripping. Look at the thick, gooey mess you've made everywhere."

I can only whimper, his words driving my arousal higher, and I feel more of my juices slip through my folds. I'm glad my flaming face is pressed against the plush, velvet backrest.

"I cannot wait to taste you," he coves over me to whisper in my ear.

A single long finger runs along my folds, then repeatedly taps against my swollen clit until I'm almost screaming, begging him to make me come.

Without further warning, Nathan gets on his knees and falls onto my pussy like a starving man, licking my folds rhythmically, taking me right to the cusp of orgasm. When my back bows and my muscles tense, he suddenly stops.

"Nathan, please, don't stop. Make me come," I mindlessly yell.

"Oh, you will." He stands and pulls down his zipper, and the sound is enough to cause a shiver to run down my spine.

I don't remember everything about Nathan, but something tells me I'd better hold on for dear life right now.

And then, I can't think anymore because the fat head of his steel-hard cock is stretching me so well, wringing out a groan of pleasure from me.

"You're going to come, Tess, thrashing on my cock." My eyes roll to the back of my head. I'm not sure what is driving me the craziest: his words or the fact that he's only pushed a few inches inside me, and he already feels too good.

By the time he bottoms out in me, my thighs are shaking with pleasure, and my skin feels too hot.

He gathers my hair in one hand and holds my waist in his other, then starts to fuck me with deep and hard thrusts, repeatedly hitting that spot inside me that drives me insane. It robs me of sense and decorum.

I get loud, begging for him to end my torture and make me come before I die of pleasure. Begging for him to never stop because it feels too good.

This time, when I reach the point of no return, he fucks me through it.

"Come for me, baby girl," he commands, but I'm already unraveling.

My orgasm hits me like a burst of fireworks exploding in the sky. "Fuck! Nathan!" I scream.

"That's it, baby. Revel in it. I've got you," he croons, wrapping his big arms around my jerking torso in a reassuringly firm hug, even as he keeps fucking me through my unending climax.

When I become aware of my surroundings again, my thighs are slick with my juices, but he's still hard as stone and thrusting inside me.

Suddenly, Nathan withdraws, and he puts me back on my unsteady feet.

"Get on your knees," he commands.

I don't need any coaxing to fall to my knees and worship the cock he just fucked my brains out with.

I taste myself on him but recognize his own essence. He's hard and hot, and oh so big. I run my tongue along his veiny length and around his sensitive head, loving the grunts I'm drawing out of him.

Feeling powerful, I wrap my mouth around his length and start to suck. He groans as if he's being tortured. His hand fists on top of the couch's headrest, his other hand returning to my hair. Pulling on the strands and rocking his pelvis into my mouth with a decadence that both shocks and arouses me, he orders me to go faster and to suck him harder.

Nathan is crazy about what I'm making him feel. He isn't just a guy getting head. There's more to it than that. I think I just found a major weakness of his.

The notion pleases me to no end as I imagine driving him insane by sucking him off over and over again until he begs me to stop.

I increase the suction and pace, enjoying the feel of him in my mouth. The raw sounds he's making get even louder as filthy words pour from his mouth, making me blush and ache for relief.

"Tess, I'm coming," he warns, gasping, and I moan, eager to taste him. My fingernails scoring his thighs trigger his orgasm.

With a shout, he starts to come, filling my mouth with his thick, salty cum. I swallow everything he gives me until he finishes.

Still panting, he pulls me to my feet but then swings me up in his arms when he sees how wobbly my knees are.

"Nathan," I whisper into his neck.

"Yeah?"

"You should know that I really, really love the way you taste."

He huffs out a laugh. "Christ, I am so fucked."

"I know, babe, you are." I giggle.

He starts walking, heading further into his house.

"Where are we going now?" I ask.

"Bedroom. I want to kiss you until either of us can't breathe, then fuck you in my bed. Then, we can carry on christening every other surface in the house if you're up to it."

My only response is to lick the tanned, salty skin of his neck, something I'd been wanting to do since I laid eyes on him at the hospital.

Chapter Twenty-Three

TESSA

I WAKE UP SLOWLY to feel warm skin against mine and my head being pillowed on Nathan's chest. His smell is intoxicating, inviting me to push my nose closer and inhale his scent.

Earthy. Familiar. Like the empty herbal tea boxes I liked to shove my nose in whenever I was chosen to help prepare meals for over a hundred other kids I lived with.

My eyes fly open, even as the thought evaporates like a mist. Where the hell did that memory come from?

I drink in my surroundings, remembering how awed I was when I first saw his bedroom with its high ceilings, large windows, and artificial fireplace. A modern replica of a bedroom in a Victorian era.

Before I can move my head, my eyes again fall on Nathan's impressive torso, and I get distracted.

God, he's fucking ripped. His skin is tanned and glowing with health. I almost can't believe I've been intimate with this gorgeous guy.

I start to trace and follow his muscled pecs, covered with dark, silky hair, and are arranged into neat swirls, tapering into a line between his abs and trailing down to his cock.

I pause when I catch myself already wrapping my hand around him. We hardly slept all night. He was insatiable, and I couldn't get enough of him, either. So, we didn't stop or even leave the bed, except for bathroom breaks.

I should let him be. He must be tired, and I don't want him to think I'm too needy. I take my wandering hand away.

"What, changed your mind?" Nathan's sleepy rasp rumbles in my ear.

"Hey." I look up to meet his blue eyes. "You're awake."

"You were touching me," he says as if that should explain it. "Don't you know that you leave a trail of fire on my skin when you put your hands on me?" he whispers.

"I should hope so." I chuckle. "My own behavior around you is way too mortifying. I need to learn how to play it cool a little bit, or at least be able to pay you back in some way."

"True," he agrees. "Every little thing drives you wild, doesn't it? You'd think I was a sex god or something."

"Don't get cocky with me. Otherwise, I'll be on you with my tweezers while you're sleeping, plucking out those grays peeking through here and there."

He laughs. "Have at it. You do know what they say about plucking, though."

"Yep. More grow in their place. Good thing I think it's so fucking sexy. Almost like you've been sprinkled with seasoning or something."

He shakes his head in amusement, then looks down at me but promptly gets distracted by my breasts. "Have you always preferred older men?" He licks a fingertip, then starts tracing my areolae.

I bite my lip but am unable to suppress a moan as my nipples tighten and start to ache.

I prefer you.

"Have you?" He nudges me for an answer.

"No. Besides, you say 'older' like you're ancient. I mean, come on, you're only eighty-nine, and you even still remember how to wear your dentures, and your liver spots—"

He bursts into laughter before he starts to tickle me until I'm begging for mercy.

When we settle, he remarks, "I'm about the same age as your father, Tess."

A flash of pain lances through me, killing all of my humor as an anxiety-inducing memory comes to me. It disappears just as soon as it appears.

"What is it, baby?"

"Um... it's nothing," I reply.

"Did you remember something?"

"I thought I did when you mentioned my father. And just before you woke up, I had a small flash. It was about an orphanage, I think. Was I adopted?"

"Yes, Tess, at age eleven."

Makes sense. I'm not sure how to feel. Relieved that I'm starting to remember? Anxious that my returning memories could somehow come between Nathan and me? I think it's a combination of the two. Then, there's the question about how exactly I ended up in the ICU.

"You're right about things triggering me, Nathan. My memory feels just out of reach, like just a scratch away from the surface. But whatever happened had to do with my adoptive father, right?"

Nathan nods slowly.

I try putting the facts together. I nearly drowned while waiting for Nathan, who I believed to be my boyfriend but isn't.

And then, my dad tried to kill me. It's awful and shocking, but I still feel numb about it, almost like it's happening to someone else, because there's no depth of emotion accompanying my revelation. It's just facts.

But even though I know that my dad had a hand in what happened to me, I don't remember all of the details. "Did he try to drown me, then?"

"No, he tried to drug you."

"Oh, wow. He must be a real asshole. Why would he do that? And how?"

"I'm sure his reasoning is somewhere in this lovely head here." He presses a kiss to my temple. "He might have mentioned something to you."

Psychopaths tend to tell their secrets to their would-be victims with the belief that they would never live to repeat the story, so I know that Nathan may be right.

"The most important thing is that he's far away and he can't hurt you anymore."

How does he know for sure? I don't want to spend the rest of my life looking over my shoulder, but the thought of something else happening to me makes me break out in goosebumps. "But what if he's looking for his victim who got away?"

Nathan looks like he's debating telling me the truth. "The psychiatrist advised us to be careful because too much exposure to the trauma could trigger an even worse amnesia for you."

"Okay. But should I be worried about my father looking for me since I don't even recall what he looks like? Is that why you brought me here?"

Shaking his head, he gathers me closer into his chest and runs his hand down my spine. "He's not exactly in any condition to be looking for you, anyway."

"What do you mean?"

"I hurt him a little bit. When I saw what he was going to do to you, I hit him. Multiple times."

"Nathan!"

"He's alive, he just needed a quick trip to the OR. I've got a few charges to face for what I did, but considering the case is a complex one with high emotions and self-defense involved, not to mention I'm also a key witness in nailing him for his other crimes, I might be able to get a plea bargain to get the DA to drop the assault charge."

My eyes are like saucers. *His other crimes. My boyfriend beat up my father to a pulp and may be facing charges, which are unlikely to stick. And I'm here with half of my memory gone. How did my life get this interesting?*

"Oh, my God, Dr. King, you put someone in the operating room! That must be like ten violations of the Hippocratic Oath or something."

"He's a serial killer, Tess. He has a unique MO, has killed other people before, and was likely to kill again. I may have saved more lives by that singular act. Think of it like trying to squash a deadly bug."

"Well, when you put it that way... I guess..."

"By the way, I told you once not to call me Dr. King. I think you need a reminder of what my first name sounds like."

His flirty tone and heated stare succeeds in distracting me. "Really! Why was I banned from calling you Dr. King?"

"Because you saying my first name makes me hard."

My mouth opens into an "O" shape. "That's a very bizarre symptom you're displaying. I think we'll need a group of experts to crack that particular diagnosis, Dr. King. I'm thinking psych." I glance pointedly at his cock. "Definitely a large team from urology, too..."

"Fine." He starts to get off the bed and motions for me to do the same. "You've asked for it. Let's go before my mom gets here."

"Wait, what! Your mom is coming here this morning?"

He nods. "She's on her way back to France, but she wants to see you again before she leaves."

"Oh, shoot! I should get dressed! What time will she get here?"

Nathan gives me a look, then gestures to his obvious erection. "And what do you expect me to do with this?"

I giggle. "I dunno, stash it under a blanket. I can't keep Caitlin waiting, or worse yet, have her overhear me screaming on her son's cock."

He shoots me a disbelieving look, his mouth slightly parted in surprise. "You must be joking. In any case, it would make *Caitlin's* entire year if she were to hear a woman screaming on her son's cock."

I can only stare at him in shock, not even sure where to start my line of questioning in response to what he just said.

Nathan cocks his head toward the other side of the room. "Move your sweet ass, baby, let's go. You and Mom can catch up after I'm done with you."

Like I can resist that body. "Okay, but we'll have to be quick."

"Whatever, it's up to you, anyway, isn't it? You can decide how many orgasms you want." He drags me up and over his shoulder.

"Hey, where are we going?" I ask as I try to push myself up against his back.

"To a place where your screams can echo off the walls while I spank you for breaking my rule."

My eyes widen. "I beg to differ. I can't be held accountable for something I have no recollection of agreeing to."

He snickers wickedly. "Too bad ignorance doesn't absolve guilt."

"Nathan, your hands are literally the size of spades, my backside is going to be in shambles!" I squeal in protest.

"Shows how much you know. Your ass has been kissed by my palm a number of times, and I can tell you that you fucking love it."

Oh, wow. He's spanked me before?

My core pulses with need, anticipating what it would feel like. "How many slaps are we talking about here?"

"Since you sassed me a lot today, at least ten. Maybe more."

"One, pal, and I will most certainly not beg for more. What am I, a masochist?"

We carry on arguing right until we get into the shower and the warm spray hits my face.

That's when my eyes open, and I feel a searing pain shoot through my chest.

Chapter Twenty-Four

TESSA

I IMMEDIATELY TURN AWAY from the spray and start clawing at my face, trying to get rid of the pungent smell filling my nostrils again.

"Tess?"

My knees buckle as I curl into a ball.

"He tried to kill me," I whisper brokenly. "He killed Ciaran, and he killed my mother."

"Aw, fuck." Nathan squats beside me and gently wraps his arm around my midriff, pushing the hair out of my eyes, the steam of the shower swirling in the enclosed stall. "What do you remember?"

I cover my head with my arms, unable to stop the vicious memories rushing against me like a flock of angry birds. Everything seems to rush out at me, even memories that I seemed to have repressed from over a decade.

Situations that didn't add up but I dismissed at the time because I desperately needed to believe that we were a normal family.

"He threw a glass of water right in my face, and after that, I only had the strength to do what he suggested. All this time, he's been wanting to kill me, Nathan. He saw us together at the Citrus Fest years ago and has been wanting to kill me since then. All those invites to Thanksgiving, to Blackwell Orchard events..."

They weren't so he could try to reconnect with me like I believed—well, more like hoped.

"Sonofabitch," Nathan curses.

"All those years, I stayed away because of what you said to me on the pier."

I was so desperate for my dad's love, even after I stopped talking to him.

If Nathan hadn't harshly told me to leave and not come back, if I hadn't turned my anger and humiliation into a singular drive to leave my past behind and succeed, John would have sucked me back into his toxicity and killed me ages ago.

I turn to Nathan and throw myself in his arms. He catches me as I break down into great, wracking sobs.

"You saved me, Nathan," I say over and over.

Chapter Twenty-Five

NATHAN

A FEW HOURS LATER, Tess is sitting in the matching high-back chair by the huge, baroque style bed, still nursing the stiff martini I made her half an hour ago. My oversize, plush terry robe swallows her small frame, and her legs are folded underneath her.

She's shivering despite the warm room and the flames licking away at the LED fireplace.

I knew that the moment where she regained her memory would be hard, but I didn't predict the chaos that would follow suit.

The two women who mean the world to me, in opposite parts of my house, both hurting deeply over the same event, just for different reasons.

I've just left Mom, who is still sobbing in one of the guest bedrooms, curled up in Lyle's arms. They were meant to return to France together, but she'd made him wait in the car while she said a quick goodbye to Tess earlier.

Unfortunately, she walked into Tess's meltdown, and we told her everything.

Mom never got over Ciaran's death. The only way she managed to cope was to never talk about him, something I was only too eager to oblige her.

And barely an hour ago, not only was she then suddenly forced to confront her son's death again, she also found out that he was murdered in cold blood.

And by the man who stole the love of Ciaran's life and broke him, no less. The same man who is the son of Albert Blackwell, the cruel man who paid a pittance for her husband's struggling farm and then turned him into a farmhand. And then, Albert had thrown her and her young sons off the farm as soon as her husband died.

As if that wasn't jarring enough, her surviving son is now in love with none other than Albert Blackwell's granddaughter. Ciaran's murderer's daughter. That Tess was adopted didn't seem to matter.

Suffice it to say, my mom didn't take it well. I had to call Lyle in when she became hysterical.

And Tess, who was already struggling under the weight of guilt she carried, completely unraveled.

I drop to my haunches in front of Tess so I can meet her gaze in spite of her bowed head. "Tess?" She looks at me, her eyes green pools of hurt.

I hold her by her hips. "You know she didn't mean those things she said, right?"

"I know. That doesn't mean they're untrue, though."

"Tess, come on. You've got me. I'm here for you, and I'm not going anywhere."

"How can you even look at me?" Tears clog her voice, and I can tell that she's trying her best not to cry.

"Baby, I love you. Nothing can change that."

She flinches as if those words have ripped into her, making her guilt and pain worse.

"My father killed your twin brother. Ciaran didn't commit suicide. He was murdered by my father."

"John isn't your father, Tess. You're not even related by blood," I argue.

"We are by law," she retorts. "He raised me for longer than your father did you. What do you call that?"

"Baby, you're not responsible for his actions."

"But I saw some of the weird things he did, and I chose to be silent rather than speak up because I was desperate for his love and approval. Like the 'smelling salt' crystals he'd hide in mom's hot water bottle sack that we weren't supposed to tell her about."

Taking in a deep gulp of air, she forces herself to continue, "I suspected they came from his labs, and he was testing their effect on her. Now, at least two people have died because of me."

"Tess, baby, please, do not do this to yourself. You were a child. You couldn't have known they were deadly or that he was capable of murder."

"How are you even okay with being with the daughter of a serial killer?"

My heart bleeds for how hard she's taking this news. She knew the facts already, but regaining her memory has made it all too personal and real for her, like she's reliving everything all over again for the first time.

"Listen to me, Tess, from day one, I've admired and respected you and what you had so much potential to accomplish. The day you told me you overheard him saying it was a mistake to adopt you was the day you ceased to be his daughter, as far as I'm concerned. I may not have realized it then, but I think I was already forming a connection with you early on, and I needed to justify that in my subconscious so I could be the mentor you needed."

She digests that information, but I can see that her eyes still retain that far away, dazed, and hurt look. There's no getting through to her. Not yet.

"Caitlin is right. I don't deserve to be the woman you choose to love."

"Baby, Caitlin is grieving the loss of her son as if it just happened yesterday. Discovering you're a Blackwell was a harsh shock for her. I promise, she'll come around. My mother loves you, Tess. She flew in from France to get five minutes with you, and afterward, it seemed like her world was set right again. I'm sure she's already regretting her outburst."

"I should go back."

I huff out a steadying breath. *Christ, this woman is stubborn.*

"Go back where? Back to your house? To Boston?"

"No, I can't stand to be in my apartment just yet. But I don't think I should stay here, either. I'll stay with a friend for the rest of my sick leave."

"Isabel?"

She nods. "You remember her?"

"Of course I remember her. Now, do *you* remember what I said about how there was no turning back when I brought you here?"

She nods again.

"And you recall what you said to me?"

"Nathan—"

"Give me one good reason why I should let you go, Tess."

"Because I'm in love with you. You've saved my life twice. Even when I didn't realize it back at the Citrus Fest five years ago, you were saving me even then. You pushed me to become more. And now that everything else is falling apart, you're the only thing I want to cling to."

"So, stay with me. Move in with me. Let me love you back."

"Don't you see? You're... too much. You're everywhere. I can't think two thoughts without them being about or related to you. I don't know how healthy that is for me—us—right now that my mind is fractured."

"Theresa, you can trust me with how you feel, even if you're not sure what that is or if you should be feeling that way. I can take it, okay?"

She looks at me, and I want to cringe at the numb, disassociated look I see in her eyes. "What if I said I wanted space right now?"

"Depends on what you mean by 'space.'"

"I just want time to sort my shit out. Figure out who I am and what the hell I'm supposed to do with all this." She gestures her hands around widely. "You, Caitlin, the police investigation and the media circus that's bound to follow, KidStation and my job, and returning to Boston to finish school. It's a lot."

I straighten. I know exactly what she needs right now, and it's not space.

Tess's assertiveness is one of the reasons I love her. Trying to wear her down will only make her dig in her heels more because she's freaking out and crippled with guilt and remorse.

So, I'll give her what she thinks she needs. *Fucking space.*

"Alright. It's a lot, I agree."

"You do?"

"Hm-hmm. Which is why you have two weeks." As soon as that time is up, I'll be coming for her.

"Two weeks—"

"That's the best I can do. I'll be leaving for West Africa with Medecins Sans Frontieres to provide medical assistance there. I should be back in a couple of weeks. Have an answer for me by then, Tess."

Her eyes go wide. I can tell she's surprised by my sudden capitulation. And beyond that is also a mix of anxiety and desire. "Um... okay. But West Africa? Isn't that too..."

"Far?" I supply.

"Dangerous!"

I shrug. "It can be sometimes. But we have a resident team there and safety protocols in place. I'll be alright, babe. And I'll be back before you know it."

She shakes her head, and her honey-blonde hair flies into her eyes. "But... but that's so sudden! How long have you been planning this trip?"

Knowing that she won't like the answer, I fight against the urge to deflect. "I always go once a year around this time. They've been expecting me for two weeks but I kept postponing it. I decided I was thinking of canceling this year's trip, but on second thoughts, this might be a good time to go."

And bid a proper farewell to the team.

Because Tess will flip once she knows where I'm going. She's all for charity, but even she would draw the line there.

I take the tumbler from her hand and down the liquor. Then, I pull her into a reassuring hug. "Listen to me, I have a lot of commitments that take me around the world, but I would never leave you unprotected, unsatisfied, or when you need me. We'll talk about what you've figured out when I return. Okay?"

She nods, holding me tightly. "Okay."

"Now, since you're looking to get clarity from Isa and Chris, you'll need to tell them everything. Are you up for that?"

"I'll have to be. They might have heard something, anyway. News of an arrested serial killer can only stay under wraps for so long."

"True. Come on, get dressed. I'll take you there."

Chapter Twenty-Six

TESSA

The next three weeks are a blur of activities. Speaking to detectives from both the Valencia and LA police departments and giving witness statements take up a good chunk of my time.

It was a good thing I didn't go back to my apartment because Diane, who lives in the same complex, has been telling me how they've been getting accosted by paps and media agents wanting information about the crime that happened there.

The whole of Valencia is in a frenzy over the rumors, and Joyce, unfortunately, seems to be caught right in the middle of it.

I imagine that she's just as clueless as I had been, given how desperately she has been trying to speak to me. When I'm not juggling police interviews and dodging the media and Joyce, I've been missing Nathan like mad.

Maddy, Isa's four-year-old girl, sits beside me at the gleaming, laminate dining table, feeding one of her dolls a crumb from her almost empty plate, chatting happily while I make non-committal noises at the appropriate times to indicate that I'm following along.

"Maddy, darling, go wash your hands, then you can come back to play before bath time."

"But, Mommy, Aunty Tessa and Mini-maddy are still having their dinner. They have to finish first."

I notice Isa's stern look, and I quickly make myself take another forkful of the pasta she made. It's one of those rare Saturdays that Isa isn't on call and has no tutorials booked, so I appreciate her going all out for dinner. I just don't have an appetite.

My dad has been discharged from the hospital and is in prison custody. I agreed to testify at his trial, and my faculty, already aware of this development, will be making adjustments for the days I need to return to LA to appear in court.

I have two more weeks before my work placement at the Fount is over, but Walter has already sent Zara in as my replacement, insisting that I take the remaining time to rest before my final semester begins.

I thought I wanted space from Nathan, that I couldn't trust the overwhelming desire to be with and give up everything for him. It's only gotten worse with the distance and every time we talk on the phone.

I played it cool for the first few days after he left for Maiduguri, only occasionally staring at the email address he gave me to contact him if I wanted him to call me.

I barely made it through the first week. By the tenth day, I got an email from Nathan about a fire outbreak that caused all flights to be grounded from the local airport.

Then, I made the colossal mistake of looking up the place he went to.

I broke, begging for twice-a-day calls until he came back.

And resolved to have a serious-as-hell talk with him about his future medical outreach destinations once he returned.

I already know that my next six months in Boston will be torture.

"Look, Mommy, Aunty Tessa is just moving food around her plate, none of it is going into her mouth," Maddy announces.

Isa, who is across the kitchen, only shakes her head in disappointment. "You specifically asked for pasta and meatballs, Tessa."

I shrug apologetically. "I'm sorry. I really was craving it at the time, but my appetite disappeared again."

She rolls her eyes playfully. "Seriously, I can't wait for your baby daddy to get back because I can't deal with you anymore."

To Maddy, she says, "Sweetie, Aunty Tessa is thinking so hard that she can't eat much, but now that you mention it, she will finish her food."

After she gives me a meaningful look, I start shoveling forkfuls of pasta into my mouth, barely tasting it but acting like it's the best food I've ever had.

As soon as I'm done and Maddy gets excused to go play, Isa turns to me. "Tessa, why on Earth did you think distance was going to give you clarity?"

"There was so much going on, and I was also scared to tell him I'm pregnant. And with his mom's last words to me, I wasn't sure how they would take it."

Shaking her head, Isa sends me an exasperated look. "You mean the woman who's been here practically every day trying to get back into your good books?"

"Yes, we're cool now, but a couple of weeks ago, we were not."

"And when is Nathan getting back?"

"It's been three weeks, Isa," I whine. "I hate it. I can't eat or sleep. I just want to be with him. But I also need to go back to Boston and finish my degree."

"As you should. But not like this. Not without him knowing just how much you love him."

"I know. But, Isa, he doesn't do relationships, and with good reason. I'm scared of losing myself in him and finding out that he can't give me everything."

And I want all of him. Desperately. Only getting a part of him would destroy me in the long run.

"So, you self-sabotage because you're scared and you feel guilty about what your dad did? You know, Nathan is a big boy and you said it yourself, he'll give you whatever you ask for. My worry is that he might just let you go if you push him away. And then, what happens when you get to Boston heartbroken and realize that he's moving on?"

Nathan wouldn't let me go.

I open my mouth to tell her that, but she interrupts me by saying, "I know every relationship is different, but running away cost me my happy ending."

"Isa, I'm sorry."

"I pushed Max away because I didn't want my heart broken by a man who may not have had it in him to commit. A bigger part of me wanted him to tear all the obstacles apart and claim me for himself and prove to me I meant more to him. It hurts that he didn't do it."

My phone rings, jarring me from my thoughts, and I peer down at the screen to see that it's Nathan.

My heart thuds painfully. It's been two whole days since we last spoke. The network connection in Maiduguri isn't the strongest; sometimes, we give up speaking on the phone altogether. I'm just hoping I can get five or ten minutes of uninterrupted time with him today.

"Hey, Nathan."

"Christ, I've missed you."

"Me too. So much. When are you getting back?"

"Baby, look outside the window."

My screech makes Isa jump about a foot into the air, and I run to the window. Nathan is leaning against his A8 with his aviator sunglasses on.

For a moment, I just take him in. I don't think I'll ever get over my attraction to him.

Isa comes over to the window, then gasps when she sees Nathan.

"Tessa, why the hell are you still standing here?"

My legs are already moving, and in the next moment, I'm running downstairs like an excited little girl and flying into Nathan's waiting arms. My lips crash into his as I greedily run my hands all over him and push them into his hair.

We're ravenous, oblivious to where we are until we hear a whistle and a cheer in the distance and break apart.

He dips his face into the crook of my neck. "Fuck space, Tess. Move back in with me. I want to be there for you and support you while you're making sense of this bullshit with your dad. I want to wear you out, put you to sleep every night, and wake up with you wrapped around me."

My heart starts to pound even as my nipples bead. "I—you don't do commitment."

He huffs out a disbelieving laugh. "Tessa, have you been around me these past few weeks? I'm so fucking hooked on you that it's insane. I'm actually worried about freaking you out at this point."

"What do you mean?"

Another catcall. Yes, Isa's apartment is in that sort of neighborhood. She has retained her apartment since med school because of the easy commute to and from work, Maddy's babysitters and playgroups, and a nearby network of single moms.

Nothing Chris says ever makes her budge about moving.

"Come on, let's go inside." Nathan takes my hand and leads me inside.

I wish we were going into my apartment, then I might be pulling him into my bedroom rather than Isa's living room. Thankfully, Isa's nowhere to be seen. As soon as we get into the house, Nathan pins me right against the door and devours my mouth in a way that leaves me slick and whimpering.

"I take it you missed me," he rasps when we come up for air.

"Nathan," I gasp, my words turning into a moan when he nibbles a path along my jaw to my earlobe. "I swear, I'm going to kill you. Do you know how many heart attacks I had when I looked the place up?" I try to sound annoyed, but it's hard when his touch is so distracting.

Nathan chuckles against my skin, his breath warm and teasing. "Isn't that why you shouldn't be Googling symptoms?"

"Symptoms, yes. Not freaking warzones, Nathan. Are you kidding me!" I pull back slightly, trying to muster a serious look, but it's a lost cause against the twinkle in his eyes.

His grin widens. "It's not as bad as it sounds. People live there, and they need help. It's actually one of my safer destinations, you know."

I gape at him, incredulous. Finally, I snap, "Well, I'd say you've helped there enough. There are plenty of other places where you're desperately needed."

"Oh, really? Like where?" He quirks an eyebrow, a playful challenge in his gaze.

I lean in, our noses almost touching, and whisper with a mischievous glint, "Take a wild guess."

Nathan's eyes darken with a mixture of amusement and something more intense, more promising. "Theresa Blackwell," he whispers. "I hope you've had enough time to think because I've got a serious question for you."

"What is it?"

There's a charged silence, and then he says, "If I told you that I wanted to make you my wife, would you run?"

I gasp, not being able to fully believe what I'm hearing. "Um, Nathan—"

"Tess, I'm not doing this space thing for one second longer. Can you just get out of the way and let me give us what we both need?"

Looking into his eyes, I find the courage to tell him what I couldn't before.

"Okay. But what if I told you that you're going to be a father? Would you still stay?"

He freezes. It's the moment of truth. If he walks away now, what will I do? How can I raise a child on my own?

Luckily, my worries prove to be unnecessary because he crushes me back into his arms. "Jesus freaking Christ. My child?" He releases me, then palms my lower belly as a look of wonder seeps into his face.

I nod, biting my lip. "Is that okay?"

"Is that okay? Are you fucking kidding me! Oh, my love, that's fantastic." He lifts me up and twirls me around while I giggle like a giddy schoolgirl.

He puts me on my feet again, then growls in my ear, "I have a confession to make, Tess. I've had this clip of doing filthy things to you while your belly is swollen with my child on repeat ever since that day you told me to keep my hands to myself while staring at my crotch like a starving vixen. I could never scrub it out of my mind, no matter how much I tried."

"Oh God, Nathan, I've got one too. I wanted to suck you off so bad that day in your office. I want to now, actually."

Nathan grins and shakes his head at me. "Of course you do, my smart, sexy, dirty girl." He looks around. "I'm sure we can arrange that, can't we?"

While I love the sound of that, I don't want Isa, or God forbid Maddy, to walk in on us. "Not here."

He groans, dropping his head into my shoulder. Then, as if something has suddenly occurred to him, he picks his head up to shoot me a sensual smile. "So let's go home, then."

"Now?"

"Right now! You can come back for your things later."

"Well, if you insist." I rear my head back and give a haughty sniff.

He rumbles in laughter. "And what about the rest of my demands?"

I know he means me being his wife. "Don't you want to be in a relationship first? See how it goes before taking the plunge?"

He shakes his head. "I don't want a trial run, Tess. I know exactly what I want. You can have a long engagement, though, if you prefer that."

Nathan has always let me set the pace. Well, except in bed, and apparently, he's had enough of that.

There are still a few things we need to discuss, however. "And what about my final semester?"

Tilting his head to the side, he looks confused, like he can't see the problem. "What about it? You can go to Boston as my fiancée. Look, we're doing this. I can't fucking think or eat or sleep without knowing for sure that you're mine. I might end up getting kicked out of the Fount for gross ineptitude if you don't put me out of my misery now."

I shoot him a teasing smile. "Oh, no, we can't have that, now can we?"

"I knew you'd see my point."

He leans his forehead against mine. While we continue gazing into each other's eyes, somehow, it feels more intimate, like a revealing of souls. It warms me to no end and triggers a buzzing in my core.

"I love you, Tessa Blackwell. More than anything. Stop fucking around and marry me already."

It feels like a dream, one I don't want to wake up from. Wrapping my arms around his neck, I nod and say, "You may call me Theresa King."

His grin is blinding. "Christ, that sounds incredible."

"I know."

"I can't wait to be deep inside you just like this, where there's nothing else between us except for what we feel."

Tingles run throughout my whole body, and I groan while picturing it. "You're making it really hard to wait until we get home, Nathan."

"Literally," he agrees, grinding his pelvis against mine.

Epilogue

TESSA

NINE MONTHS LATER

"They're both asleep. Finally." I look up to see Caitlin returning from the nursery as I sift through various proposals from high school charity teams looking for support or seeking funding from KidStation.

I heave a sigh of relief. "You're a miracle worker, Mom. I can never get them to sync up like you can."

"It's just a bit of experience," she says with a twinkle in her eyes.

"I wish you could stay here forever."

"Well, make another set like those two, and I'll consider it," she teases.

I throw my mother-in-law a horrified look. Having twins once has been enough of a trial, albeit rewarding, but I can't imagine adding two more kids into the mix. At least, not anytime soon.

She seems to consider the idea as well, because she laughs and shakes her head. "Actually, on second thought, maybe not."

She heads toward the kitchen. "Now that the twins are down for the count, Tess, how about some profiteroles and a mug of black tea?"

"Oh, yes, please."

"Coming right up," she says, chuckling at my excitement.

She just made me lunch two hours ago. I'm not particularly hungry for a snack yet, but I eagerly accept.

When Caitlin offers tea, it's not just tea—it comes with quality, hilarious gossip, and sensational tips. She's always full of interesting stories, likely thanks to her frequent travels, her wide network of sophisticated friends, and just being an amazing person.

I see where Nathan gets his caring nature from. I don't know how I would have managed my pregnancy and the twins without Caitlin. But as attentive as she was, even she called me an "adorable mutant ogre" by my third trimester.

As if my regular need for Nathan wasn't enough, my pregnancy cravings were off the charts—and to my utmost embarrassment, they were all about him. His smell, taste, and his calm dominance.

So, Boston was every bit the nightmare I imagined because he was always out of reach, and video calls simply didn't cut it.

Things improved as soon as I got the nod to complete the last half of my semester online, given how close I was to giving birth. But Nathan had to work. I still cringe remembering how clingy I was just before Skye and Hazel were born.

Caitlin and Lyle practically took turns keeping me company while Nathan was at work, but they'd vanish the moment he came home. Then, I would shamelessly gorge on my husband.

I'm finally starting to feel normal now that the twins are a little over two months old, and I've started planning a fresh project, although most of my work is from home.

KidStation has been a huge success. While Zara managed the project during my coursework, I returned to find that demand had skyrocketed.

We needed to expand, and that required significant investment and creative strategies. Since I was planning to start my own NGO in LA anyway, Walter had agreed to sell me the full rights to KidStation.

Caitlin returns with tea and snacks, prompting me to set aside my laptop and pick up a steaming mug. "So," she begins, "it's been a whirlwind of events since the wedding, one thing after another."

"You're right," I agree. "We literally haven't slowed down."

Nathan and I were married in a small ceremony just days after my college graduation. The past nine months have flown by—settling into married life, dealing with a twin pregnancy, starting my NGO, attending frequent court hearings, seeking closure through my mom's journal entries, and navigating individual and family therapy sessions have all taken their toll on me.

"Just the other day, I had breakfast with Nathan. Our first in months," she reveals.

"Really! I thought you guys did that at least once every month."

The bond between Nathan and Caitlin is so beautiful that Lyle and I would never dream of interfering.

A pang of sadness hits me as I recall when Nathan first told me about his twin. I can only imagine how close they were.

I didn't understand at the time why my mom coming between them was such an issue. Now, after thinking about it, it would be cruel to try to break that kind of bond.

"So, how did it go?" I ask.

"My God, I could hardly recognize my son. He's happy, sure, but the transformation in these last few months..." She shakes her head as a soft look enters her eyes. "Tess, he's been alone for so long. When he lost Ciaran, it was like he lost a part of himself."

"How so?"

"Well, Ciaran was the broody one, a chip off the old block, while Nathan was always the life of the party—quick to smile, quick to laugh."

"Like his mom," I chuckle.

"True. It was... good to see the old Nathan back. And I know that I have you to thank for that."

I incline my head in modesty, unable to hide my happy grin. "I really haven't noticed much change in him, though."

"I think it's because you got the whole package from the start. You didn't miss anything. He couldn't really keep any part of himself away from you. But I lost those parts, and it's great to have him back." She grasps my hand. "You're the perfect partner for him, Tess."

Tears spring to my eyes. "Thanks, Mom. That means the world to me." Especially since there was a time when she thought the opposite, even if it was brief.

We sit in companionable silence for a few minutes, holding hands, each lost in thought, wistful smiles on our faces.

I think Caitlin has chosen today to tell me about reconnecting with her son because somewhere in the Criminal Courts

Building, John Blackwell is currently being sentenced for his crimes.

I stopped attending the trial after giving my testimony; it was too harrowing and it stirred up feelings of guilt. Like I should have seen through him, said something to the police earlier.

The most shocking part of the trial was the discovery that there were three other victims he'd murdered in a similar fashion.

One of his ex-girlfriends, an employee, and his younger cousin, Abel Blackwell, whom we all thought had died of carbon monoxide poisoning in his garage.

I made the decision to separate myself from the proceedings from then on.

Nathan, on the other hand, felt closure in seeing the end of the man who tore his life apart. Besides, he'd taken a plea bargain to help convict John in exchange for the dropped assault charges, so he needed to see it through.

As for the "lab," it's been raided by the government. Extensive tests are being conducted on CX3, with ongoing investigations and arrests being made.

Apparently, for the past few decades, the Blackwells have been secretly distributing the substance on the streets. While large doses could be lethal, in small doses, it's been found to render victims passive and easily influenced—a sinister and potent means of control.

The courts wisely decided to keep this information away from public knowledge, fearing it could spark widespread outrage but also interest among those with a malevolent desire for control.

Caitlin squeezes my hand. "It'll be over soon, darling, and then, all of us Kings can put this whole sordid mess behind us."

Her emphasis on our name doesn't escape me; she knows how much I've struggled with being a part of the Blackwells.

I nod in response, unable to swallow past the large lump in my throat to verbally reply.

"Now, time for a subject change. Did I ever tell you about the French sex therapist a friend of mine met in Dubai?" Caitlin starts.

Of course, I know by now that her stories are never about a friend. They're always her experiences. "Oh, my God, spill!" I urge, sitting up straight. "Did you guys…?"

"Well, that was before Lyle, and I was much younger then," she says, as if issuing a cautionary preface to her juicy tale.

Raising an eyebrow, I ask, "How much younger are we talking?"

She sniffs, caught in a playful fib. "Like a year ago," she admits.

I burst out laughing.

She dives into her tale, but our laughter is soon interrupted by the front door opening.

It's Nathan.

I look up, and I marvel because he still has the power to take my breath away. He stands tall and broad, his crisp, white shirt contrasting sharply with his dark hair, which is peppered with hints of gray on both temples. His smile broadens when he sees us both.

Glancing at the tea and snacks, he teases, "Extra juicy gossip today, Mom?"

Caitlin stands to embrace him. "Well, today's extra special, isn't it?" She lets him kiss her cheeks, then heads to the nursery, leaving us alone.

Nathan approaches me with a smooth grace, and I wait until he's close enough to pull me into his arms.

I go eagerly, wrapping my arms around his shoulders. When he feels me straining to get even closer, he knows what I need and instantly hauls me up while I wrap my legs around his waist, basking in his familiar embrace.

"Are you close enough now?" he teases.

"Hmm, yeah." I smile into his neck, not even feeling the tiniest bit self-conscious about my need and love for him.

"How are you, baby?"

"Good." I inhale his skin. "Better now that you're here."

"Skye and Hazel?" he asks.

"Sleeping for the past half hour. They both went down minutes apart, would you believe it? Your mom's a miracle worker."

"Of course she is. Ciaran and I gave her plenty of experience."

"I'm sure." I chuckle wryly. "So, what's the sentence?" I ask about the final hearing.

He exhales deeply. "Life without parole."

I close my eyes, overwhelmed by the wave of emotion. It's no surprise, considering the unanimous guilty verdict and the pre-sentencing hearing's details. "And how was that for you?"

"It won't bring Ciaran back, but it holds someone accountable for his death."

I hug him tighter, offering him comfort the one way I know how. "Do you ever think... if John didn't have the CX3, perhaps...?"

"Mary would surely have left him for Ciaran. Who knows, maybe she wouldn't even have married him in the first place."

"And I wouldn't have been adopted by them. We might never have met," I muse. "You could have been with someone else."

"Hmm. But as it happened, life broke me. I wasn't looking for love until Fate concocted my personal brand of crack and shoved her under my nose."

I cheekily retort, "You mean shoved her onto your big cock."

Nathan chuckles, shaking his head. "Theresa King, what am I going to do with your dirty mouth?"

"I don't know." I murmur suggestively, "You could try washing it out with your—"

His palm connects with my butt in a hard smack, and I squeal in pleasure.

"That's it. That's exactly what we're doing. Right fucking now."

Giddy laughter bursts out of me as he practically jogs us toward the bedroom.

And since we're being bad today, I might as well break all the rules, so I can get the punishment I deserve.

I reply, "Well, well, Dr. King, we're eager today, aren't we?"

THE END

Thanks for reading!
If you enjoyed this book, please consider leaving an honest review on your favorite Amazon store

Want more books like this?
Start Here with ***Hello Billionaire Beast***

Acknowledgements

I want to say thank you to my absolute rock of a man Shawn, and to Kaitlin Travis, Thea Louise Santiago and Muskaan Khan.

I couldn't do this without you guys xx

About the Author

Judy Hale delights in creating steamy romance novels with exciting, yet relatable characters.
She has a particular weakness for dark and twisty dominant alphas with vulnerable sides, and strong sassy heroines, just the perfect type we need to handle those men…
If that's right up your alley, then you've found the author you've been searching for!
When she's not writing, she's devouring a good romance book with a glass of mulled wine, or swimming laps.
Stay in the know by subscribing to her Newsletter
Follow her on Facebook

Also By Judy Hale

NEW YORK BILLIONAIRES
Wanted By The Billionaire
Hello Billionaire Beast
The Nanny's Bossy Billionaire
The Damaged Billionaire's Obsession

Printed in Great Britain
by Amazon